Falling for a Drug Dealer

-A Story W
Melikia G

Copyright © 201 by True
Published by True Glory Publications LLC
Facebook: Melikia Gaino
Join our Mailing list by texting TrueGlory at 95577

This story is a work of fiction. Any resemblances to actual events, real people, living or dead, organizations, establishments or locales are products of the author's imagination. Other names, characters, places, and incidents are used fictitiously.

Cover Design: Michael Horne
Editor: Kylar Bradshaw

Acknowledgements

First and foremost, I would like to thank my lord and savior Jesus Christ for given me the strength and creative mind to write what I have. I cannot wait to see where this road takes me and what else He has in store for me. I'm more than nervous about venturing out into the world of writing, but I have faith that the road traveled will be a great one. Where there is faith there should be no worry.

I would like to thank the Gaino and Williams/Mabry family for their love and support and never letting me give up on a dream. I LOVE YOU ALL!!!

I would also like to thank you the readers for supporting me on my first book and taking the time to read one of my favorite creations.

Table of Contents

Chapter 1   1

Chapter 2   6

Chapter 3   11

Chapter 4   17

Chapter 5   23

Chapter 6   26

Chapter 7   33

Chapter 8   39

Chapter 9   48

Chapter 10   49

Chapter 11   54

Chapter 12   58

Chapter 13   62

Chapter 14   70

Chapter 15   76

Chapter 16   81

Chapter 17   91

Chapter 18   96

Chapter 19   101

Chapter 20   107

True Glory Links   111

Falling for a Drug Dealer

Written By:

Melikia Gaino

CHAPTER 1

THE MEET UP

Lisa waited for her friends at the bar at Ruth Chris Steakhouse, where they do their outing that happens every month, sometimes twice a month. As Lisa sat and waited, she noticed ten minutes has passed, Lisa looked up from her cell phone and saw her two late ass friends, Kim and India, stroll up to the bar. Kim gave Lisa a hug while India flirted with the bartender to get her a free drink. While India is flirting with the bartender, Tracey and London walked in.

Tracey looked over at India and said, "Damn bitch, you always flirting and shit."

India turned around while rolling her neck and eyes and replied, "Fuck you bitch."

Lisa turned to everyone and exclaimed, "Where the fuck is Danni and Lorren?"

Kim replied, "Yea London, call your sister and find out where the fuck she at... like now!!"

London left the group to call her sister, while Kim sat down in a chair to call Danni. After getting off the phone with Danni, she said, "She parking."

Then London walked back and said, "Lorren told us to go ahead and get seated because she had to take lil Rico to my mother's house."

1

Meanwhile, Kim went up to the hostess and told them they were ready to be seated. As soon as she finished talking, Danni walked in. She hugged Kim and said, "I'm sorry for being late, I got a little side track." Kim understood and signals her friends to come on.

As they sat down at the table, the waiter asked, "What would you lovely ladies like to drink?"

Danni said, "Apple martini."

Lisa said, "Strawberry daiquiri."

India said, "You! If that's ok?" with a slight grin.

Lisa said, "Stop playing India, we hungry."

India said, "Damn, I would have a Sex on the Beach and your number." The waiter smiled and winked at India.

Tracey said, "Screw these soft ass bitches, and give me some Goose, straight up, no chase."

London, laughing hysterically, replied, "Call me soft then, bitch, cause I just want an Apple martini."

Kim said, "I would also have an Apple martini with a glass of water too."

After the waiter took the drink orders, the girls started talking about what was new. London started off by telling them about a new design that she had to make for her class and that she planned on having her dream house built. Then Kim chimed in and started to talk about one of her patients fucked up mouth that she had to work on today.

Kim said, "Y'all that bitch breath stink… I was about to drown her ass with mouth wash. Then my damn adviser trying to

2

act like her breath didn't stink. Then she had a fucked up grill, teeth missing and everything."

As Kim told her story about her day at dental school, Lorren walked up to the table and asked "What's so funny?"

Danni said, "Kim telling us about this bitch who mouth she had to work on."

A few moments later, the waiter brought the drinks to the table and asked, "Are you all ready to order?"

Everyone replied, "Yes," in unison. Everyone ordered steak, but as always Kim had to order something different which was salmon.

Tracey said, "You always have to be different you uppity bitch." As always, Tracey got a 'fuck you bitch' from Kim.

While the ladies waited for their food, they talked more about their jobs and school. Then out of the blue India ask Danni "Why were you late?"

Danni looks at India and said, "I lost track of time. Any more questions?" She looked around the table.

Then Lorren said, "You got it pimping, she was just asking a question." The whole table started to laugh.

After dinner it was still early, so London came up with the idea of going to happy hour at club passion, which was downtown. Everyone was down, but Danni and Lorren said they had to go.

"You know ma would watch Rico for you while we go hang." London said trying to convince her sister to come out with them.

Lorren looked at her sister then huffed and said, "I know, but I don't want to leave him with ma too late."

Kim said, "Don't worry Lorren, we ain't going to be out too late cuz I have to wake up early."

Feeling confident that they have convinced Lorren, all they had to do was convince Danni.

Then Lisa said, "Danni, why do you have to go home so early? We all have to wake up early!"

Danni looked at her friends and said, "Don't worry about it, and let's go have some fun!"

When the girls were about to leave out of the restaurant, Kim noticed that India wasn't with the group. She rode with Kim, so Kim asked Tracey if she saw India. Tracey said "That bitch probably getting some man's number."

Then out of nowhere India said, "No trick. I was using the bathroom, thank you very much!"

Then they all got in their cars and headed to Club Passion. Once they parked their cars, they went right in the club and headed for the bar. Once they were at the bar, they order drinks after drinks and they partied like they didn't have class or work the next day. All of a sudden, Danni gets a call on her cell phone and it was her boyfriend, Bryon. He wanted to know where she was at and why she wasn't home yet. Once she got off the phone with Bryon, she hugged her girls and said she had to go. Everybody's boyfriend seemed to all be thinking alike because they called and asked what time were they coming home. The only person whose phone didn't ring was Lisa. So everyone said their good bye and headed their own way. But before they left, they all planned to log on AIM at 5p.m. as they did every day.

Each of these girls were smart and driven. They all graduated from Johnson C. Smith University and now enrolled in graduated school or dental/medical school and have great jobs in their field of study. India was a political science major, who is in graduate school at Maryland University and works at a law firm part time. Tracey was an education major, who was enrolled in graduate school at Howard University and work as a cosmologist teacher. Danni was a biology major, who is in medical school at George Town University and working as an assistant obstetrician/ gynecologist at Georgetown University. Lisa was a social work major, who attends graduate school also at Maryland University and works as social work intern. London was a computer engineer major, who is also in graduate school at George Washington University and works as an engineer. Lorren was also a social work major, who is in graduate school at American University and works at an elementary school as a counselor. Then there was Kim, who was also biology major and is enrolled in dental school at Howard University and works as an assistant dentist.

CHAPTER 2

HOW THEY MET (5 years ago)

It was a hot ass day in Charlotte, where the friendship of a life time emerged. As the freshman moved into their dorms, parents and students were everywhere. As Kim made it to her dorm, she looked for her friend Lisa that she attended high school with. Lisa and Kim knew each other for a while and were excited to be in the same dorm. So as Kim walked in her room she met her roommate Tracey. Tracey was also from the same area as Kim, so they had something in common. As their parents left, Kim and Tracey got more acquainted. Then there was a knock on their door. So Kim went and answered it and it was Lisa.

Lisa said, "Hey bitch, it took you long enough to get here."

Kim said, "I been here for your info. I was trying get my shit together. Anyway, this is my roommate, Tracey. She is from our area too."

Lisa said, "How you doing Tracey? I'm Lisa!"

Tracey said, "I'm good! It's nice to meet you!"

"So who is your roommate?" Kim asked while putting her clothes in the closet.

"Some girl named, India. I think she is from our area too." Lisa said while sitting on Kim bed.

While they sat and joked around in Tracey and Kim's room, Lisa asked Kim to walk with her to her room. Kim agreed and they both walked to Lisa's room, leaving Tracey to unpack. Once they walked into Lisa's room, her roommate India had the music jamming and with two girls in there. Lisa and Kim walked in the room and India asked, "Is the music too loud?"

Lisa said, "No, its fine!"

Kim being the more outspoken said, "Shit, that music is too loud."

Lisa hit Kim on the arm and said, "Don't mind my friend! This is my friend, Kim, she don't have any manners!"

India looked Kim up and down then said, "This is my friend, Danielle, but we call her Danni and this is her sister, Staci."

Everyone greeted each other. But, India kept giving Kim a slick looks because she didn't like the fact that Kim tried to get smart with her. They started talking and asking each other where they were from. While they were getting acquainted, Kim's cell phone rang. It was her cousin, Jasmine.

Jasmine was Kim's cousin from Virginia. She was smart as shit but she was such a thief. Jasmine could steal your shirt off your back and you wouldn't even know it. Jasmine was so slick with everything that she do that she got everything for her dorm room by making a fake credit card. Jasmine and Kim were very close. Many thought they were sisters, but they only saw each other during the summer time because they lived so far away.

Kim answered her phone, "Hey Jazzy Jaz, where you at?"

Jaz said, "Hey cuz I'm checking in, ma is down here and want to see your ass."

Kim said, "Here I come." Kim told Lisa that she would be back she was going to meet her cousin, Jasmine.

Kim went down stairs and spoke to her aunt and gave her cousin a hug. As soon as Jasmine's mom left, Jaz went and showed her cousin everything that she had got with her fake credit card. After she showed her all of her stuff, they went back to India and Lisa's room.

After a while of getting to know each other they became closer.

The next week... first party of the year!

Jaz, Kim, Tracey, Lisa, India, Danni, and Staci got ready to go to the first party of the year, which was a Kappa party. The girls were dressed to kill and ready to get it in. When they arrived at the party, the girls were pumped up and ready to dance. India, being the freaky one, was dancing with all of the dudes in the party. She didn't give a fuck if their girlfriends were there or not. Right next to her dancing was Kim. They were getting their man on, when this girl approached India.

"Yo, you was all up on my man!" The girl said to India.

"And your point is?" India asked back with attitude.

"I don't like when bitches dance with my man that is my point." The girl said back to India.

"Well, I think you need to talk to your man, cuz clearly he came behind me." India said.

The girl looked at her friends, who walked over to India with her. "This little bitch thinks she is funny."

Before she could even get the chance to turn her attention back to India, Kim came out of nowhere and punched the shit out of the girl in the face. Once that happened, India followed up with Tracey, Jaz, Danni, and Staci right behind her. While they were fighting in the club, a girl named, London, who didn't like the girl neither, took it upon herself to jump in the fight. When Lorren, London's twin sister, saw her in the fight, she jumped in it ready to get down with the get down. They were fighting for a good ten minutes before security came and kicked the whole crew out. Lisa was the only one who wasn't in the fight and still got kicked out. She was on the other side of the club dancing and was trying to get to the fight, but when she got there everybody was getting kicked out of the club.

All of the girls' hair looked wild and they were so pumped up that they wanted to wait for the girls to come out of the club. They wanted to fight some more.

"I like how you just stole that girl, Kim." India said giving Kim a high five while they waited for the shuttle to get a ride back to school.

"Yeah, I had to do it, that bitch was talking too much. She wanted beef she got it." Kim said.

"Yo, who are y'all?" Tracey said towards the twins, who jumped in the fight.

"I am London and this is my sister Lorren." London said.

"Why did you jump in the fight?" Jaz asked.

"I can't stand that bitch. Her fucking boyfriend was trying to talk to me and she came stepping in my face. I was going to whoop her ass at school, but I didn't want to get kicked

9

out so I was waiting for a chance when we meet up off of campus." London said.

"I just jumped in it cuz that's my sister." Lorren said letting everyone know that she had her sister's back.

"Where the fuck was you Lisa?" Kim asked laughing.

"I was dancing and when I tried to get in the middle the fucking security was throwing y'all out." Lisa explained her whereabouts.

"Well y'all know we got beef now on campus. They going to try us every chance they get. So I guess we are a crew now." India said.

All of the girls agreed and from that day on, they were known as the baddest chicks from DC. Their saying was "WE DA BADDEST." They didn't take shit and didn't anyone give them any problems. Their friendship are still strong and they are more sistahs than friends.

Chapter 3

London & Lorren

London and Lorren Smith are the craziest twins in the world. London is the oldest by three minutes, but she acts like she's Lorren's mother. London is the more controlling one; she can talk anyone into doing anything. Her friends call her the con-artist. While London is the more controlling one, Lorren is the outgoing one. Lorren is calmer than London but loves to joke all the time. She doesn't have a problem saying what is on her mind. The twins have a younger brother, whose name is Landon. Landon looks nothing like Lorren nor London, but everything like their grandfather. The twins are caramel complexion, while their brother is dark skin. They all got their height from their father and their hair from their mother. They were raised by their mother, Lacey, and father, Donny. They grew up very comfortable because Donny, also known as Don, was a well-known hustler. He hustled to support his family. He moved them in a big house and made sure his children had money to go to college. When the twins were in their last year of middle school, their father was killed. After his death, their mother became secluded toward her children. The twins had to look after their brother and each other. They had to grow up faster than they wanted and London took on the responsibility of caring for her mother, sister, and brother. After a couple of years, their mother finally realized that she was being selfish towards her children, so she became the mother she used to be. Their father had hustled so much that their mother didn't have to work and the children didn't want for anything. Landon had a lot female tendencies due to his confusion of how men were supposed to act. He grew up around his mother and sisters, so that was all he was used to. Throughout their young lives, they endured a lot of hardships, but they were able to overcome them with their strong family structure.

London

London was dating this dude named Keith. London met Keith at an engineer convention at Ohio State University. He was six foot two inches, light skin, long braids, hazel eyes, and a sexy ass goatee to match his full lips. Keith is a real smart and clean cut dude. He cherishes the ground that London walks on. London and Keith had been together for three years. They met when they were juniors in college.

Now, they live together and are having problems.

"Keith, where the fuck you been at all day? You know we had plans!" London yelled at him when he walked through the door. She was pissed off because he had been coming home late lately.

"Yo chill... I been making money, I had to work late."

"Whatever nigga, you get off at 5 and it is 10p.m. Are you cheating on me nigga?"

"No girl... why do you always thinking that I am cheating on you?"

"Maybe because we don't spend time with each other no more and when we have plans you pull this shit."

Keith laughed at London and said, "You know I love you and won't disrespect you like that. If you want to know where I was, I'll let you know sweetie."

London looked at him with a serious look and said, "Nigga, I'm not laughing, where were you? Cuz if you were with some other chick I'm going to cut your balls and dick off."

"You need to calm your ass down, cuz you not going to do nothing. Anyway I was with my boys, I honestly forgot about our date. I'm so sorry baby. I love you!"

"So your boys are more important than me?"

"Hell no baby! I forgot. I don't complain when you out with your girls all damn day. I forgot one date and you ready to cut a nigga balls and shit off. Do you love me?"

"Yes, I love you."

"Do you trust me?"

"Yes, I trust you"

"Well, stop acting like that and come over here and give me some pussy."

London smiled seductively and walked over to him, and started kissing him. He picked her up while kissing her and started heading for the stairs. Once they got to the bedroom, he placed her on the bed and started to put in work. Keith was known for his master tongue skills. He proceeded by kissing her thighs and moving upwards. Once he hit the spot that he was looking for London closed her eyes and enjoyed the pleasure that only her man brought her with his tongue. Keith noticed that she was enjoying the treatment so he wanted to tease her. He stopped and watched her reaction. London was trying to pull his head back between her legs but he wouldn't go until she said, "Finish what you started, now nigga." He loved when she talked controlling towards him.

"So you want me to keep going?" he asked while he teased her.

London was getting more upset and wanted him to keep going. She wrapped her legs around his neck and would let him come up for air until he continued his assault.

When he was able to get up for air, he turned her over and entered her rough. London screamed with pleasure.

"Who pussy does this belong to?" Keith asked.

London screamed out in pleasure and said, "It's your... this is your pussy."

"Are you going to stop tripping?"

"Oh Yes!"

"Are you ready for me to cum?"

"Yes! Cum with me!"

They both exploded together. After they got their rocks off, Keith held London while she dosed off. While London was sleep, she heard the phone ring.

"Hello." Keith said half sleep.

"Hey Keith, where is my sister?" Lorren asked.

"She sleep, Lorren." Keith replied.

"Well, can you wake her up? It's important."

Keith shook London and told her that her sister was on the phone.

Half sleep London. "What's up?"

"I can't deal with this nigga no more."

"What he do now?"

"This nigga got the nerve to ask me why I took my son to my mother's house the other day when we went to the club and out to eat. He had the nerve to say that I know you and your hoe ass friends were at the club shaking y'all ass."

"You know he all talk. He didn't put his hand on you did he?" London asked her twin ready to go over to her house.

"He is not stupid! He is just talking crazy! He had the nerve to say if I try and leave him he would kidnap me and lil' Rico. I have to get away from him before he decides to hurt me and my baby!"

London had heard enough and told her sister, "You and little man can come and stay with me until you find a place of your own."

While London was on the phone with her sister, Keith was listening to the whole conversation. After she hung up, that's when the fussing began.

"Why the fuck you tell her that she can stay here?"

"Don't question me nigga! That's my motherfucking sister and nephew, and if I wanted my whole family to stay in my house then they could."

"This is my motherfucking house, London, and I don't want no damn bad ass baby fucking up my shit. You know me and your sister don't get along."

"Oh well, get over it cuz they will be here tomorrow and you not going to start no shit, and that's the end." London glared

15

at him and turned her back as she cut the light off on him, without saying good night.

Chapter 4

Lorren

I hate the fact that I had to call my sister in the middle of the night with my problems. But I just couldn't talk to anyone else. I have been going through a lot of things with the love of my life. His name is Rico Rodriguez; he is Puerto Rican with long wavy hair. He is about six foot three inches tall, muscular, and the sexiest lips you have ever seen. I love Rico, but he is too crazy and deranged for me. This is not the first time he threatened to kill or kidnap me. The first time he told me he was going to kill me was when we found out that I was three months pregnant and I told him that I wasn't ready for no baby and I was going to get an abortion. That time he begged me to have his baby and I did because I loved him so much. We been together since they were 17 years old and we couldn't be any closer. He is really jealous and not afraid to show it, anywhere we go.

Last week, when I went to hang with my girls and sister, he had the nerve to get mad at me. I had told him two days before that he had to watch RJ, but his dumb ass went to leave out talking about 'I got to go make some money, your ass don't need to go out anyway!' He just makes me so mad.

Lorren was on her way home from school and picking up her son when her cell phone rang and it was Rico.

Lorren breathed heavy then answered the phone, "Hello."

"Where in the fuck are you?"

"I'm on my way home. Why are you yelling?"

"You know your ass supposed to be home an hour ago. You got me waiting around for your ass and shit. You think your ass slick too."

"What are you talking about Rico?"

"I know your ass went to Club Passion! Didn't I tell your ass you didn't need to go out? Stay your ass home with my motherfucking son."

"Look, I had plans anyway he was good. He was with my mother."

"I don't give a fuck, Lorren. You his mother, he only supposed to be with you. And you know I don't like my son being around your gay ass brother."

"You know what, fuck you Rico! I can't take this shit anymore."

"Where the fuck are you?"

"I'm pulling in the drive way." Lorren said with attitude. He just hung up on her. She was pissed.

When she got her stuff and RJ out of the car, they headed to the house. They lived in a very big house that he bought when he had found out she was pregnant. That was two years ago.

As soon as she opened the door, Rico was sitting in the TV area watching ESPN, calm as the ocean acting like he just didn't go off on Lorren a few minutes ago. RJ loved his father and looked so much like him.

"Daddy, daddy, daddy!" RJ yelled once he entered the house.

"What's up little man?" Rico asked his son, that he loved so dearly.

"I made you something, while I was at grandma's house." RJ told his father, excited to see what his father would say about the picture he made for his father.

"Really? Go bring it here!" RJ took off toward his room where his mother took his book bag to get the picture he made his father.

While RJ was looking for the picture he made, Lorren went into the kitchen and started putting up the little bit of groceries that she got from the store. While doing so, Rico came into the kitchen.

"Who you get all sexy for?" He asked Lorren.

"No one."

"Yeah tell me anything. If I ever find out that you cheating on me, I'm going to kill your ass Lorren."

"Whatever! You ain't going to do shit. You just a bunch of talk nigga."

"Try me if you want, Lorren." Rico said. As he was walking close on Lorren, RJ came into the kitchen and saved his parents from a rumble.

Rico looked at his son and said "let me see the picture little man?" RJ gave him the picture and explained it to him. While he was listening to RJ, Lorren mumbled to herself, "I have to get away from this jealous, derange, bipolar ass nigga."

While Rico entertained RJ, Lorren was in the kitchen cooking dinner for the men in her life. She cooked and fixed their plates. Then she told them to come to the table and eat. These were the times when Lorren loved her man. He was a great father towards little Rico due to the fact that he didn't have a father figure. RJ looked at his mom and said, "This is yummy."

She smiled at her son and said, "Thank you baby."

Being the bipolar person he is, Rico said, "Yeah its good ma. But next time don't take all day coming home to cook for your men."

Lorren just looked at him and continue to eat. After they finished eating, Lorren went to run RJ some bath water and gave her son a bath. After taking care of her son, she cleaned up the kitchen. Then she went to the master bedroom. Once she went in there, she didn't feel like being bothered with Rico's crazy ass so she just went right to the bathroom to take a shower and got ready for tomorrow.

Rico saw her walk upstairs' and laughed to himself because he knew she was mad at him and was going to just go to bed on him. He wasn't having that though because he ain't got any from her in a while and he was horny as shit. So while Lorren was in the shower, he walked up and opened the curtain and he just stood there and looked at her for a minute then he grabbed her roughly and pulled her towards him.

"Are you mad at me?" he asked Lorren, she didn't say anything.

He started to kiss her neck and ask her again "Are you mad?"

Not facing him she says, "Yes, I hate when you talk to me like I'm not the mother of your child or the love of your life."

"I'm sorry baby, I know you not doing anything when you go out with your people, but I just don't want anyone to look at what is mine."

"You make it like you don't trust me, Rico?"

"I do trust you. Promise you won't take my son away from me."

"I won't, but you scare me and I don't feel safe around you sometimes."

He placed his hand between her legs and started to message her clit. "Am I scaring you now?"

Breathing heavy, she said, "No, I feel safe."

While working his fingers, he asked her, "If you love me, why were you planning on taking my son from me?"

His hands were feeling so good that she was in another world. Moans escaped her mouth and she said, "I couldn't take you no more so I was going to leave."

He was mad, but he wasn't going to let his anger escape and scare her into leaving him for real and taking his son. So he asked her, "Do you still want to leave me?"

She said, "No I'm not going to leave you."

"That's what up! Now come here and give your man some of his pussy!"

She turned to him and they started in the shower and moved to the bed where they made love for the majority of the night. After they finished, Rico got up and took a shower.

"Rico, where are you going?" a half sleep Lorren asked.

"It's time to make some money. You know that."

Lorren was upset that her man had to go out and sell drugs and couldn't hold her through the night like she wanted. But she knew that was the life of being a hustler's wifey.

Chapter 5

Lorren and London

It was 7:00a.m. And Lorren had to get up and get herself along with little Rico together when her house phone rang.

"Hello." Lorren said.

"So what's up? Are you moving out that house?" London asked her sister.

Lorren knew her sister was going to be upset with her answer because she didn't like Rico. But she loved Rico and didn't want to mess up their family even though he is a little crazy. She took a deep breath and said, "No he apologized and I'm going to stay here."

"You know you can be very dumb at times." London said not hiding her disappointment.

"I don't have time for this London. I have to go." Lorren said and hung the phone up before her sister could respond.

London

"I know that bitch did not just hang up in my ear," she said out loud in her office.

She couldn't believe that her sister was being so dumb. She needed to talk to someone so she called Lisa.

"Hello, this is Lisa Davis." Lisa said when she answered her office phone.

"Hey Miss Prissy, I know you ain't doing no work. So what are you doing?"

"For your info Ms. London, I do have work to do today. I have a paper that is due at six." She laughed.

London laughed because she knew working and school was a lot. And most of the times while they are at work they do homework to make it look like they're doing work for the office.

Lisa could sense something was wrong so she said "What's wrong London?"

"It's a lot Lisa. I don't know where to start?"

"How about you start at the beginning?" Lisa said with a slight laugh.

"Well it's like this, I think Keith is cheating, Lorren is stupid, and Landon isn't trying to help ma with the house bills. My family is going crazy."

"Why do you think Keith is cheating? Why is Lorren stupid? You know Landon is a moocher and is lazy. He always been like that and I don't think he is going to change." Lisa explained.

"Keith's been coming home late. When I call him, he don't answer his phone, we hardly have sex anymore. If his phone rings, he acts all suspects. I don't know what to do. Secondly, he went off when Lorren called last night about staying with me for a while."

Lisa had heard enough. "The way I see it is that he is doing something, but I really don't think he is cheating cause that boy loves you too much. Why do Lorren want to stay with you?"

"That crazy motherfucker is tripping again. But I just got off the phone with her and now she is going to stay with his crazy ass."

"It's your sister's life, you can't be mad at her. She would have left him sooner, but she don't want to strip RJ of a father."

An understanding London decided it was time to change the subject. "Have you talked to Kim and them?"

"Yes girl. I talked to that damn crazy ass India. I talked to Kim last night, but she wasn't feeling well." Lisa said in a concerned voice.

"I' m going to call and check up on her today. What was India talking about?" London asked because India was the wild one who always had a story to tell.

"She was talking about this guy she had sex with last night and that his penis was so little. I don't know why India insisted on telling me about her sex life when I don't even have one." Lisa said. Lisa was the virgin of the group and she wasn't big on dating either.

London laughed and said, "She tell you stuff because she know you is a virgin."

London and Lisa talked for a while. Then they said they would catch up soon and said their good-byes.

Chapter 6

Kim

Kimberly Williams was raised by a single parent. Her father was killed when she was five years old. She had a little sister named, Angel, and an older brother named, Malik. When their father passed, Malik was nine and he idolized his father. Growing up, Malik saw how much his mother struggled trying to pay the bills and keep the children happy. Malik loved his mother and sister more than anything, so when Malik turned fourteen, he began to hustle. He would hide his earnings from his mother and pay her bills on the sly. He even would buy Kim some outfits and tell her to don't tell their mother. When Kim was thirteen and Malik was seventeen their mother had Angel. Their mother was dating this dude named, Aaron. He was an average dude and when he found out that Mia was pregnant, he left her. "I don't want any children" is what he told her. Malik already didn't like Aaron from the start, so that just made him angrier when he found out that his mother was pregnant. Malik continued to hustle even harder to make sure the women in his life were set for good. Kim used to be on her way to school and see Malik on the block and use to ask him "Can I stay with you?" He used to walk her to school because he needed his sister to make something out of her life. He was more of a father to her than a brother. He was there for her first date to the time she went to college. He was extra overprotective of his sisters and mother. He was still that way till this day.

As Kim lay in bed not feeling well at all, her phone would not stop ringing. She thought about cutting off the ringer but she didn't want to miss Shawn's call. Shawn was her boyfriend, who was so sexy. He was six foot four inches tall, nice body, caramel complexion, hazel eyes, nice close cut with waves, and then he had lips to die for. Kim is five foot four inches tall with reddest brown skin with curly hair, she has the most beautiful smile with deep dimples, with hips, ass, and she has a sporty figure lean with a nice shape. Most people mistake her as being Native American. Shawn and Kim had been together for four years. She met him when she was in undergrad and she came home for a break, and they been together since. He is originally from New York but moved to DC to be with Kim. Kim and Shawn have the relationship that a lot of people envy. Kim is going to dental school, while Shawn is a drug dealer. She worries about him a lot but she knew what he did when she first met him.

Lately, Kim hadn't been feeling well and Shawn was gone to New York for a 'business trip.' She had been feeling sick since Saturday. She just got off the phone with her friend, Lisa. Lisa thought that Kim might have food poison and told her to go to the doctor tomorrow. While Kim was laying in the bed, her phone rang again.

"Hello." She said weakly.

"What's wrong with you hoe?" Tracey asked.

"I'm not feeling well. What's up?"

"I was calling to see if you wanted to go to the mall with me today. Since I called your job and they said your ass took off."

"I just told your ghetto ass that I'm not feeling well." Kim said then laughed.

"What is wrong with you?"

"I think I have food poison. My stomach hurts so badly, and I feel weak."

"Oh damn man. I'm going to bring you some soup and ginger ale today when I get off."

"Thank you. I'll be here." Kim said to Tracey. Then they hung up.

After getting off the phone, she tried to get up and do some homework but was too weak to get up so she just laid in the bed and fell asleep. She was awakened by a knock at her front door. Kim wasn't going to answer it because all her friends and her man had a key. So she just laid there while they knocked. Then she heard the front door open, she was too weak to move so she just turned over to see who came in her house.

"I know your ass is not still in the bed." A loud Lorren said when she entered Kim's room. Following her was RJ, London, Lisa, India, and Tracey.

Kim just looked at Lorren and her friends and said, "I'm too weak to get up. Anyway why are y'all over here?"

"We came over here to check on you and bring you something to eat." Lisa said being the concerned person she is.

"Thanks y'all." Kim said. She looked at RJ and told him to come here. She loved RJ as if he were her own son.

"Hey auntie, are you not feeling good?" RJ asked.

"No baby, I'm not feeling good today. I have something for you." Kim told RJ. She always gave him gifts. She gave him a new toy car.

A smiling RJ jumped off the bed to go and play with his car and tell his auntie thank you.

While the girls was chilling and talking, Kim's phone rang.

"Hello." She answered with an attitude.

"Hey ma, you called me?" Shawn asked.

"Where have you been? Why haven't you been answering my calls? Where the fuck you at?" Kim question Shawn.

"Yo what's up with the attitude ma? You know where I been."

"Whatever nigga! Why haven't you been answering my calls?"

"I didn't get no call from you ma, Now what's wrong?"

"If you would have been answering your phone you would have known that I been sick since Saturday."

"I'm sorry ma. I'm on my way home! Do you need anything?"

"Nope my friend's came to take care of me since my so called man is out doing God knows what."

"Don't start it Kim. I'll be home shortly." After Kim got off the phone with Shawn, her friends wanted to know what he was talking about.

The girls talked and laughed for a while and then India asked, "Where is Danni?"

Everyone said they haven't talked to Danni since they went out to eat.

So they called Danni's phone, no answer. So India called Danni's sister, Staci. Staci hadn't seen or talked to Danni. While the girls sat around, trying to figure out where Danni was, Shawn walked through the bedroom door. He looked around and greeted all Kim's friends then gave Kim a kiss on the forehead.

"Hey ma, you feeling better?" Shawn asked.

"A little, thanks to my friends." Kim said not hiding that she is mad.

"I'm going to watch TV down stairs, let me know if you need me." Shawn stated then he left the room and took RJ with him.

When he left the room, all eyes went to Kim because she slightly cursed him out in front of all her friends. Kim looked around and said, "What y'all looking at?"

They all just burst out laughing. Tracey looked at Kim and said, "You is a show."

While the girls chilled, India's phone rung and it was Danni. Danni told India that she had been busy and she was alright. After the girls finished catching up for another hour, they decided to leave. They all said good-bye to Shawn and told him to go tend to Kim's sick ass.

He walked through the door and stared at her. Kim just continued to watch TV. Shawn sat on the bed next to her and continued to stare at her. Shawn said, "I'm sorry baby. I love you; let me take care of you."

"I just want you to hold me Shawn. I hate that you always hustling." Kim started crying.

Shawn asked, "Why you crying?"

"Because I don't know if you going to come home or not, then you don't answer when I call."

"I'm sorry! I'm going to do better." He said, while holding her in his arms.

When she dozed off, he got up and took a shower and made her some soup. When Kim woke up, Shawn was in bed watching TV and on the phone. When he noticed Kim was up, he said "How do you feel beautiful?"

She smiled at Shawn and said, "I feel a little better." She got up and went to use the bathroom and when she came out he was off the phone.

"Your mother called!" Shawn said. He was looking at Kim weird. Kim noticed the stare.

"Why you looking at me like that?" Kim asked.

"I think you might be pregnant, ma."

"Why would you say that?"

"You got a glow to you, all of a sudden you real emotional, and you feeling tired all the time." Shawn stated.

"I just been sick, I'm not pregnant."

"Ok ma, you know your body."

Kim didn't want to talk about the possibility of her being pregnant because she knew she could. She and Shawn had been kind of reckless with the 'pull out' method.   So she went and picked up the phone to call her mother.

"Hey ma! You called me?"

"Yeah, I was just checking on you."

"I'm doing fine." Kim told her mother.

"Well, my son-in-law said you were sick."

"I am but I feel better. Any who how is that sister of mines? Have you talked to Malik?"

"She's good for now, getting on my nerves every damn chance she gets. Yeah, I talked to him the other day he said he is going to make a trip and see you."

"Oh ok. I'm going to talk to you tomorrow, ma."

After getting off the phone with her mother, she walked over to Shawn and they started to get busy. He hadn't had any in a while and Kim hadn't either. They missed each other so much. After they made love he looked at her and said, "I still think you pregnant." He kissed her forehead and held her till she fell asleep.

Chapter 7

India

India Scott was raised by both parents. India is dark skin, very slim, long hair, and perfect teeth. India was known as the black Barbie. Unlike her friends, she went to private school and had the good life. She has only one brother, who is Jonathan, and both of their parents went to college. India was spoiled and likes to get her way. She was a daddy girl. Her father and her brother spoil her so much. India's been spoiled since she was young; but when she got in her third year of college, her father informed her that he was cutting her off because she needed to learn how to defend for herself. India was so use to being soiled that she started to sleep with dudes and they would take her out and buy her whatever she need and wanted.

India was at work doing nothing when she received an IM from her friend Kim. India read what Kim wrote. Kim was telling her that she wanted her to go to the doctor with her after they got off. India agreed and they ended the conversation. When 3:00p.m. approached, India called Kim on her cell phone.

"Hello." Kim said through the phone.

"I'm off now, I'm about to change my clothes and come and scoop me up."

"Why I have to drive? I'm the one who's sick." Kim said not in the mood to drive.

"Alright, I'll come and get you with your sick ass." India said and then hung up the phone.

Once India made it home, she checked her machine. She had a lot of messages from the men she had slept with or tricked. India didn't want to talk to any of them, so she went to her room and changed her clothes, so she could take her friend to the doctor. After changing her clothes India left right back out the house and drove to Kim house. When she arrived at Kim's house, she beeped the horn and Kim came out.

Once Kim got in the car India said, "Which doctor's office you going to?"

"The one uptown" Kim replied.

They pulled into the parking lot of the doctor office. Kim signed her named and took a seat next to India. "So what do you think is wrong with you?" India asked Kim.

"I have no idea. I couldn't even stay awake at work today. That's why I asked you to go to the doctor with me." Kim responded.

While they sat there and talked, the nurse came out and said, "Ms. Kimberly Williams." Kim and India stood up to go in the back. Once they went to the back, the nurse took Kim's weight and other measurements. She then led her to a room where she asked her to change out of her clothes into the provided gown.

After changing in the gown, her and India were laughing and talking when this sexy six foot man walked in. Both Kim and India sat there and looked up at him with a stuck face.

"Hey ladies, I'm Doctor Lloyd." Doctor Lloyd said.

"Where is Doctor Rose?" Kim asked. Wanting to know where her normal doctor was.

"Doctor Rose is out of town and I'm filling in for her until she returns." He stated.

"Ok. I'm Kim and this is my friend India."

"Nice to meet you both." He said smiling at the both of them, but lingering on India.

While he was washing his hands, India leaned over and said "He is so damn sexy. He is going to be mines by time you finish with your check up."

Kim laughed at her friend and said, "Go for it girl. At least he is doctor, so you know he getting paid."

"Ok are you ready, Ms. Kimberly?"

"Yes, let's just get this over with."

"So, what is wrong?"

"My stomach has been hurting and I think I have food poison."

"Well, let's see what is going on?"

While the doctor examined Kim, her phone rang and India answered it.

"Hello." India said.

"Yo, which one of the crew members is this?" Shawn asked.

"This is India. What's up Shawn?"

"Where is Kim?"

"The doctor is examining her right now. I will tell her to call you when she done."

"Aight shawdii, peace."

While the doctor was still examining Kim, India started to flirt with him.

"So, are you married Dr. Lloyd?"

"No, I'm not married and no I don't have a girlfriend either."

"Oh so can I get your number, and you take me out to eat or something, so we can get to know each other a little better?" India asked seductively.

"Yes. I can give you my number and take you out anytime that you might be available." Dr. Lloyd said back and smiled at her.

"Oh trust and believe, I'm ALWAYS available boo." India replied.

He turned his attention back to Kim and the monitor where he was doing a sonogram. Then he saw a figure that appeared to be the size of a pea on the screen. He examined her a little more and gave her the news that he ultimately knew she saw.

"Ms. Williams, I'm looking at the monitor and if my calculations are correct, you are about two months pregnant."

Kim turned her head to the doctor, and then turned her head to India. Lastly she looked at the monitor. She stared blankly at the small figure on the screen. A million questions began to run through her mind but the one that stuck out the most was the fact that she was going to be a mother in less than seven months. Kim had stared at the screen for so long that she didn't even notice the tears that had begun to stream down her face.

"Why are you crying honey?" India asked Kim.

Kim didn't respond, she just continued to cry. India walked over and hugged her friend who needed her support more than anything. While they hugged, Dr. Lloyd excused himself from the room. After Kim got herself together they made an appointment to do a follow up exam and left. India took Kim home because Kim wanted to be by herself for a while.

As soon as India got in the house, her house phone rang.

"Hello." India said through the phone.

"What's up sexy? Can I see you tonight?" Bryant asked.

"No not tonight, I have to study."

"I don't want to take you nowhere; I just want to get some pussy. A nigga been feigning for that shit."

India, who is not shocked by his response, replied, "I have someone coming over tonight, so not tonight."

"You ain't nothing but a hoe anyway. I don't see why I keep fucking with your trick ass." Bryant said before hanging up in her ear.

India went into her room and started to study for her test that she had the next day. She really didn't have company on the way, she just didn't want to be bothered with that little dick ass nigga. After studying, she checked on Kim who informed her that she was ok and she was going to tell the girls and Shawn

about her unexpected package at Tracey's cookout which was
this weekend.

Chapter 8

Tracey

Tracey Johnson was tough, ghetto, and so real. She was raised by her father and had three older brothers whose names were Troy Jr. also known as TJ, Tyler also known as Ty, and Tony also known as Tone. Tracey's mother left their family when she was two years old. Tracey is the splitting image of her mother. They both have light brown skin, slant looking eyes, which made her look like she was mixed with Chinese. She has curves like her mother and everything. Tracey was about five foot four inches tall and a little firecracker. She had a mouth like a sailor, and was so hood. Her father and brothers raised her to be that way, but they also made sure that she learned how to survive and not want from no one. They gave her lessons on surviving in the street along with keeping her grades up in school so she could become something in life.

Tracey was getting ready for her birthday cookout. It was a hot ass April day and Tracey's birthday was Sunday, so she wanted to have a cookout with the people she loved. Tracey was about to leave out the house to go get the rest of the stuff for her party when the phone rang.

"Hello." Tracey said a little frustrated.

"You have a collect call from Zoe." The operator said.

Tracey and Zoe had an off and on relationship since they were in junior high school. They grew up together and were madly in love. Tracey went through break up, jail and even cheating with Zoe.

"Yes. I will accept the charges."

"Hey baby! Are you coming to see me today?" Zoe asked happy to hear the woman of his dreams voice.

"Naw, I'm not going to be able to make it today, I'm having my birthday cookout."

"Yo you know you ain't told me no shit like that. You got a nigga waiting for your ass and you ain't even coming to visit a nigga."

Tracey didn't feel like fussing so she said, "How about I try and see you tomorrow?"

"Whatever you say Tracey. Anyway my cousin told me he saw you with some punk ass square nigga."

"Man, don't start no shit with me Zoe. I was not all up in some nigga face. I don't know why your ass getting mad. You did the dumb shit to get you locked up." She stated to remind him that he was locked up.

"Don't start it. You still my woman don't be fucking that punk ass nigga."

"Whatever player, you don't run anything. I got to go so I'll try and see you tomorrow."

After getting off the phone with Zoe, her phone began to ring again. She was now agitated with the phone ringing and she was trying to get out the house.

"Hello." She answered with a slight attitude.

"Hey baby! Are you ready to get the stuff for your party?" Kenny asked.

Kenny was Tracey's boo. Kenny and Tracey met in college and they became friends when she was having a problem with Zoe. Ever since that day, he talked to Tracey and helped her with her problem with Zoe, they had been close. Kenny was in love with Tracey, but he knew she was in love with Zoe, so he would rather be her friend than nothing at all. Kenny and Tracey had sex occasionally and he took care of her. He pays her bills, car note, and her schooling. He owns his own business and is an account major. The only reason why she wouldn't date him is because she loved bad boys and she thinks Kenny is too much of a "chump."

"Yeah, I'm ready, are you outside?"

"Yeah, come on baby girl."

Tracey gathered her stuff and headed out the door. Once she got in the truck, he leaned over and gave her a kiss. They went to the store where they got the rest of the food and drinks for the party. On their way back to her house, Kenny looked at her and said, "Baby, do you want your birthday gift now?"

Tracey just looked at him and said, "Sure why not."

He opened the glove compartment and pulled out two plane tickets. He handed her the ticket and she was shocked to see a flight for tomorrow to Jamaica.

Shocked Tracey says, "We going to Jamaica tomorrow? OMG I can't believe it. I don't have any outfits or anything. What am I going to do?"

"Whoa baby, hold with all the questions. Yes we leave tomorrow at seven in the morning, I'll take you shopping when we get there and don't worry, just enjoy your birthday with Me." Kenny said so smooth.

41

After making it to Tracey's house, they began to set up for the cookout. Around seven that evening, people started to show up at the cookout.

The first of her girls to show up was Lisa as usual. Lisa came to the party with her younger brother, Larry. Larry was seven years younger than her and he wanted to party. When they walked in, they greeted the birthday girl. Just then Lorren, Rico, London, and Keith came in together. When they entered the party, the guys went to speak then went straight to the bar.

Tracey looked at the twins and asked, "Y'all rode together?"

Lorren looked at her and said, "The ride here was a trip. You know can't none of us get along so it was a car full of people who can't get along."

They all laughed at Lorren because they knew she was telling the truth. While they were laughing, India walked in by herself. India's motto was 'why bring sand to the beach.' India was looking for more dudes to recruit. She came over to the group of girls, and asked, "Did Kim get here yet?"

Everyone looked at her weird then Lisa asked, "Why are you looking for Kim?"

India responds quickly by saying, "No reason."

After saying that, Staci, Danni, Taye, who is Staci's boyfriend, and Bryon walked in the party. Everyone came over to Tracey and spoke.

Taye looked at London and asked, "Where is Keith?"

"He is at the bar." London replied.

After the guys left to head to the bar, they began to catch up.

Lisa looked at Staci and said, "I haven't seen you in a while. Where you been hiding?"

"I just have been busy at work and at school." Staci replied.

While Staci was catching the girls up on her where about, Kim, Shawn and Shawn's friend Kevin walked in and everyone turned to them.

Kim walked over to her friends and said, "Hey y'all and Happy Birthday Tracey. This is for you!" Kim gave Tracey a gift. Shawn gave each of the girls a hug, and introduced them to his friend. As soon as Shawn introduced Kevin to India, she was giving him the eye.

After everyone got aquatinted with each other, the guys left and went to get a drink and mingle with the other guest.

India leaned over and whispered in Kim's ear, "How do you feel? Did you let Shawn know yet?"

Kim looked at India and whispered, "I'm doing better and no I haven't let him know yet."

London looked at Kim and India whispering and said, "What's the whispering for?"

Kim just looked at her and didn't say anything. Lately, Kim had been bitter towards everything and everybody so she decided not to answer London's question right then.

Tracey walked over to Kim and put her arm around her shoulder and asked, "What's wrong, sweetie?"

"Really not in the talking or partying mood." Kim replied, "Nothing I'm not feeling too well."

"I know when something is wrong with you Kim, so what's the deal?" Tracey asked.

Kim eyes began to water and then she said, "I'm pregnant."

Lisa came over to Kim, hugged and wiped her tears. "Don't cry. Does Shawn know that you're pregnant?"

"No I haven't told him."

London looked at Kim because she was upset that Kim didn't tell them that she was pregnant and hadn't told her boyfriend that she was pregnant. London looked at Kim and said, "How many months are you?"

"I'm two months."

"How long do you plan on hiding this pregnancy from your boyfriend and when were you going to let us know?" London was talking to Kim as if she was her child.

Kim was too drained and didn't feel like getting into it with London so she just walked towards the house. When Kim left, Tracey looked at London and said, "Bitch you're wrong for that."

London looked at Tracey and said, "What did I do that was so wrong, Tracey?"

"You know that girl is pregnant and right now she need our support, not your smart ass comments." Tracey said.

India looked at both of them and said, "First of all, Kim was going to let all you know today. While we are sitting here fussing and shit, Kim is in the house crying and she isn't ready to tell her boyfriend, so I think it's her decision. So I feel we need to keep it that way."

Lorren walked away from the group and went in the house to find Kim. While Lorren was talking to Kim, Tracey saw Shawn walking towards the remaining girls. He looked for Kim and didn't she her anywhere.

"Yo Tracey, where is my baby girl?" Shawn asked Tracey.

"Umm she went in the house she isn't feeling too well." Tracey replied.

"Ok. Yo India keep my man company while I go and look for Kim." Shawn said to India.

Shawn went off to find Kim, meanwhile the party is still live and everyone was having a good time.

Kim

"Kim, are you ok, honey?" Lorren asked a crying Kim.

Kim looked up and saw Lorren standing over her as she lay in the guest room. "Yes, I'm fine. I've just been so emotional lately and I don't know what to do."

"It's going to be like that for a while, but you'll learn to cope with it." While Lorren talked to Kim, they heard Shawn's voice calling her name.

"Do you want me to let him know what room you in?" Lorren asked Kim

"Sure, I'm going to have to do this sooner or later." Kim said.

Lorren walked out the room and informed Shawn where Kim was at.

"What's wrong baby?" Shawn asked concerned with his woman.

She started to cry again and he rushed over to her and held her. Then Kim looked at him and asked him, "Do you love me?"

"You know I love you, so what is this about?"

"Would you ever leave me?"

"No I would never leave you, ma. You are starting to freak me out. What is it, ma?"

"I'm pregnant." She said and began to cry again.

Shawn just looked at her and a smile came across his face. Then he said, "That's nothing to cry about. I'm so happy. We are having a baby. That's why you been so emotional and sick?"

Kim just looked at Shawn, who was so happy that a smile came upon her face. "Yes this is why I been emotional and why I have been keeping my distance from you."

"How many months are we? Why you didn't tell me? When did you find out?" Shawn asked a million question before Kim could answer.

"We are two months, I didn't tell you because I wasn't sure how you would react, and I found out the day I went to the doctor, which was Wednesday. India took me."

"So that's why India called you a million times checking on you?"

"Yes."

While the party was going on, Kim and Shawn started getting prepared and accustomed to the fact that they had a baby coming in seven months.

Chapter 9

Tracey after the party

The party was off the hook. The night of the party we found out that my girl Kim was two months pregnant. Rico got drunk and he started to argue with Lorren. Danni tried to take a drink, but Byron wouldn't allow her. I think he beats, her but I'm not sure. Lisa turned down at least five guys. London and Keith was bunning up all night. India that girl is so nasty I think she fucked Shawn's friend, Kevin, in my house because those two did a disappearing act. Staci, I'm not sure about her because she kept going to the bathroom and every time she comes out her eyes are glossy. I think the girl is on drugs. I had a great time. Kenny couldn't have thrown a better party. I'm thinking about making him the main man in my life. Shit, at least he takes care of me. I know if I do that to Zoe he would be hurt, and plus Kenny hasn't shown me any signs of being hood. He seems like someone I can take advantage of and sometimes I need a ruff neck. I guess I just have to wait till we go on this Jamaica trip to see how ruff he would get with me. If he can do that, I may just tell Zoe good bye. Now, I have to go and give my boo some pussy cause he so rightfully deserves it.

Chapter 10

Lisa

Lisa Davis was born in the projects. Out of all her friends, Lisa had it the hardest. Lisa was born to Tonya. Tonya was known around the projects as being a hoe. Lisa never knew who her father was. Tonya was on drugs for a majority of Lisa's' life. When she was seven years old, her mother had her brother, Larry. Larry was Lisa's pride and joy. While Tonya was out doing drugs and tricking, Lisa was home trying to fend for herself and her brother. She was thirteen when she started to develop. She was always a looker, so when she got older, all type of dudes tried to get at her because they thought she was like her mother. Lisa was light skin with hazel eyes and hips that she got from her mother. One day while Lisa was home taking care of her brother and doing homework, her mother was out looking for drugs and one of her Johns' came to the house. He tried to convince Lisa to have sex with him, but Lisa pulled out a little gun that she got from her friend. The man left after he saw the gun. After that happened, she couldn't live like that anymore, so she called her great grandma and told her what happen. She loved her mother to death but she refused to be a victim to one of her tricks anymore. Since that day, she lived with her great grandma who took good care of her, and that was the day she promised to never be like her mother and to never have sex until she was in love.

Lisa's alarm clock went off at 7:00 a.m. She was tired from the party yesterday but she never missed church. After she got out of the shower, she went into the other room and woke her brother Larry up so they could make it to church. Even though he knew that Lisa was his sister, he respected her as if she was his mother. Their grandma had custody of them since Lisa was thirteen and Larry was six. Unfortunately, their grandmother passed when Lisa graduated from college. Her brother was still a minor so Lisa took it upon herself to adopt her brother.

"Wake up boy!"

"Yo I'm up. Dang Lisa, you act like we going to be late." Larry said to Lisa while pulling the cover over his head.

"Boy, don't make me slap you on this Sunday."

"Ok. Lisa I'm up. Are you happy now?"

"Matter of fact I am."

Lisa watched as her brother got out of the bed and headed to the bath room. The only thing she could do was shake her head. Larry is sixteen about to turn seventeen but looked like he was around twenty-one years old. He stood at six foot tall, light skin with cornrows, and also had hazel eyes. He was the spitting image of Lisa almost.

An hour later, Larry and Lisa were headed out the door to church. They made it there on time. Larry was a heart breaker in the church. All the girls wanted to talk to Larry. Meanwhile, Lisa only had her eye on the pastors' son, Darnell. Lisa was so in love with Darnell that she wanted him to be her first. The only thing was that Darnell was a hoe.

"Good Morning Sister Davis." Pastor Jones said to Lisa.

"Good Morning Pastor. How is everything today?" Lisa asked.

"I can't complain. He woke me up today and started me on my way. I'm blessed and highly favored."

"Amen pastor."

The church service was off the hook. The choir tore it up and the word was even better. After the service, Lisa was happy to see Darnell. He was a cute, brown skin thing. He had a low cut shape-up, a Rick Ross goatee, the most gorgeous set of straight pearly whites, and the body of a GOD. Not to mention the brother smelled great.

"Hey good looking." Lisa heard the deep voice.

She turned around, smiled and said, "Hey. How you been?"

"I'm doing well now that I see you. When are you going to let me take you out?"

Lisa was shocked because he never asked her out, and Lisa wasn't used to being asked out anywhere. So she replied as if she was India. "You can take me out anytime you want too."

Darnell smiled and said, "I'm going to call you later on sweetheart."

Lisa couldn't control the blushing. Lisa and Larry went home. The first thing she did when she got home was log in to AIM to see if any of her girls were online. Not to her surprise they all were except for Tracey who was in Jamaica, celebrating that birthday of hers with Kenny. She put dinner on and went straight to the computer to get advice from her friends who was much more experienced than her.

"Hey girls, what's up?" Lisa typed as she opened up the chat room.

"Nothing, I'm just reading some notes for class tomorrow." London wrote.

"I'm watching TV with RJ." Lorren wrote.

"I'm on a date with the Kim's doctor, Dr. Lloyd." India wrote.

"I'm just lying in the bed." Kim wrote.

"How are you going to be on a date and IM us at the same time?" Kim asked India.

"I'm on my phone dumb ass." India wrote back.

"Anyway I need some advice." Lisa said.

"What's up?" London asked.

"Don't y'all remember Darnell that go to my church?"

Everyone typed, "Yeah we know who Darnell is."

"Well today he asked me out on a date. Y'all know I really like him and if everything goes right I want him to be my first." Lisa stated.

"First you need to go on more than one date with this boy before you start talking about losing your virginity to him." Lorren wrote.

"I know. I don't know how to act around him. I get nervous and I don't know what to talk about so I make a fool of myself when I'm with him."

"First you need to think like me. Know you the baddest. Have an attitude that makes him want you, not you wanting him." India wrote.

"LOL if you act like India on the date Lisa, you are bound to get fucked that night!" Kim wrote.

"I would have to agree with Kim on that one." London wrote.

While they were giving Lisa advice, Danni finally signed in.

"Hey y'all. What's up?" Danni wrote.

Everyone then turned their attention to Danni because she was always late with everything. First they started asking where she had been at. Then they filled her in about what they had been talking about.

"I'm thinking clubbing this weekend." India wrote.

Everyone agreed to go clubbing on Saturday. When they finished helping Lisa, they logged off and went their separate ways.

Lisa went back to the kitchen and prepared dinner for her and Larry. After they ate, Lisa went to her room to get ready for her day at work, while Larry went and talked on the phone to one of his "lady friends".

Chapter 11

Danni

Danielle Moore also known as Danni was brown skin, gray eyes, shoulder length hair, and a great body that a lot of woman wants. Danni always has been a looker, but she falls in love easily. Danni was born in a fair neighborhood. She was raised by both parents. The only flaw of their household was that Danni's father use to beat her mother. When Danni was eleven years old, she found out that she had a sister named, Staci, who was her father's love child. Danny cheated on his wife with Staci's mother, Stephanie. Stephanie and Danny used to do drugs together. After Mary found out about her husband's other child, she didn't want to be married to him anymore, so she put him out to live with his baby's mother. Danny lived with Stephanie for two years and then he moved to a richer neighborhood where he had a house and a new girlfriend. Danny was a good father to his girls, so he kept them every weekend so they can grow up knowing each other and knowing their father. Even though he did drugs sometimes, his girls would never know. Danny was known as a rolling stone. Danielle got her nickname Danni because she was a daddy's girl and they looked just alike. They have the same facial structure and eyes. Staci had her father's smile and nose. All three of them have the same brown skin.

Danni was at the house getting ready to go out to the night club with her friends. The girls decided to go to Club Passion, which was their usual spot because they never had to pay and get in. While Danni was putting on her hipster pants and her low cut shirt, her boyfriend Bryon walked in the room.

He kissed Danni on the back of the neck. "Hey beautiful"

"Hey honey. How was work?"

"It was long and stressful. So where are you going looking all good?"

"I told you the other day that I'm going to club with my girls today. You said it was fine if I went."

"Oh yeah, I almost forgot. So you don't want to stay home and take care of your man. I just told you, I had a long and stressful day." Bryon asked taking his shoes off.

"I really wanted to go out, but if you want me to stay I won't go to the club." Danni said looking at Bryon.

"Well, since you about to go out and hang with your friends, can I get a kiss?" Bryon asked.

Danni walked over to her man, who was now sitting on the bed and leaned in to kiss him. He kissed her, and then out of nowhere he punched her in the stomach. Danni curled over in pain. He then proceeded to kick her in the stomach repeatedly. Danni was on the ground crying in pain. All of a sudden, he stopped his abuse on her and looked at her cry.

Then he said, "Go ahead and go to the club with those hoes that you call friends. Next time, I won't be so nice." Then he walked out the door and left Danni crying in pain.

After he left the room, Danni sat on her room floor crying. Not sure what her next move would be. She didn't know if she wanted to stand her girls up again or leave to go to the club and expect an ass whopping when she got home. Danni wasn't sure if she stayed home if Byron would continue to beat her, so she decided to leave before he came back upstairs' and used her as a punching bag.

While Danni was in the car on her way to meet her friends, she had to make sure nothing was visible of the ass whopping that she just got. When she pulled in front of the club, she saw all her girls there waiting for her. Danni was always late because she had to cover up the abuse from her friends.

"Hey ladies, I'm so sorry I'm late."

"That's nothing new." India said.

"Let's go get our party on." Tracey said.

The group of girls walked in the club and they always was in VIP. They were VIP because Kim's cousin, Jasmine, was dating the owner Marcus. Marcus was an ex-hustler who took his money and made a night club.

"Ladies, what would it be tonight?" The bartender asked.

"Goose and cranberry juice." Tracey said.

"Blue motorcycle." replied London.

"Patron straight." Danni said.

"Goose and cranberry juice." Lorren said.

"Apple martini." Lisa said.

"Virgin strawberry daiquiri." Kim said not feeling the sober outing.

After the girls received their drinks, they went to the VIP section for a little while, and then India was ready to hit the dance floor. India, London, Lorren, and Tracey went to the dance floor. Danni, Lisa, and Kim stayed in the VIP sipping on their drinks. Danni was drinking to numb the pain from her beating. Lisa always drank light, and Kim was pregnant.

"Why are you drinking so heavy, Danni?" Kim asked.

"I had a long day and needed a drink."

"Oh true." Kim said.

They were looking at their friends dance and get there mans on. Then a group of sexy dudes from out of town walked to VIP. Kim noticed a brown skin dude, who was six foot three inches tall, sexy smile, hazel eyes, five o clock shadow, long braids, and a nice figure. She couldn't help but smile at him. He took that as a sign to come over. When he came over, he brought his crew with him.

"Hey how are you ladies doing?" The one giving Kim the eye said.

Everyone replied fine.

"I'm Quan, these are my niggas, Moe, and Terence." He said.

Moe was six foot four inches tall, caramel complexion with long dreads, a smile that would light up the day, and his swagger was off the hook. Terence was six foot two inches tall, brown skin with a low haircut, a neatly trimmed goatee, and perfect white teeth.

"I'm Kim and these are my girls, Lisa and Danni."

Kim told Quan she couldn't talk to him because she was in a relationship. So they just exchanged numbers and he told her to call him when she is free or need someone to talk too. Danni on the other hand was feeling her drink and was flirting with Moe really hard. Lisa was just talking to Terence and gave him her number. After the guys got their numbers, they left.

Chapter 12

In the Club

As the DJ was getting the club crunk, Kim had just left the bathroom and was making her way back to the VIP section. When she arrived to the VIP, she noticed that Lisa was talking to the guy Terence. She sat down and drank her strawberry daiquiri, leaned over, and asked Lisa, "Where did Danni go?"

"She on the dance floor with the rest of them hoes." Lisa replied.

As the girls danced, Kim was so busy drinking her strawberry daiquiri that she didn't notice Shawn standing in front of her. He seemed heated because she was in the club.

"Yo ma! What are you doing in the club?" He asked.

Kim looked up and realized that Shawn was standing in front of her. "I'm just chilling with my girls."

Lisa stopped talking to Terence and looked at Shawn and Kim. "Hey Shawn, how you doing?" Lisa asked.

"What's up Lisa, I would be doing better if my pregnant girlfriend wasn't in a club. By the way, what the fuck are you drinking?" Shawn said to Lisa, and then directed his question to Kim.

"It's a virgin Strawberry daiquiri. You would have known that I was going to the club if you didn't run the street all damn day. If I see you more, you would know my whereabouts." Kim said.

"Whatever, it's time to take your ass home."

"I didn't drive so I'm leaving when my girls are ready."

"Naw, we both leaving." Shawn grabbed Kim and they exited the club.

When Kim left the club with Shawn, the rest of the girls were getting their freak on. India was on the dance floor freaking some dude, when she felt someone pull her. When she noticed that it was Kevin, Shawn's friend that pulled her, she tried to get away from him. India never told any of her friends that she and Kevin had sex at Tracey's house during the cookout. They had a session in the basement on top of the washing machine. India gave it to Kevin so good, now he calls India all day long. He was really feeling India even though he knew she is a hoe.

"So you don't answer your phone when I call?" Kevin asked India while holding her hips tight and grinding on her as the DJ played slow songs.

"It's not like that, Kevin. I'm not trying to be in a relationship right now." India said enjoying the feeling of Kevin grinding on her.

"I understand what you saying, ma, but I'm letting you know now that you going to be my wife."

"So, is that right?" India asked.

"Yeah, but you won't even let a nigga take you out or come over and wine and dine you."

"You can take me home tonight." India said, letting him know that she wanted some from him.

He smiled at her and said, "That's all a nigga asking for."

Meanwhile, Danni was having a great time dancing with Moe. Then all of a sudden her cell phone rang and she knew right off the back that it would be Bryon. So knowing that it was Bryon calling, she excused herself from Moe and went to answer the phone.

"Hello." She said, barely able to hear over the noise.

"When are you coming home? I'm sorry for hitting you earlier. I just get a little angry when you want to go out with your friends and don't want to spend time with me. Plus, you was looking to sexy." Bryon pleaded over the phone.

"I understand baby. I'm on my way home now." Danni said.

"Ok I got a surprise for you when you get here." Bryon said.

"Ok I'm leaving as we speak." Danni hung up the phone, ready to see what Bryon got for her.

After Danni told everyone she was leaving, Lisa got a call from her brother Larry. Lisa had told Larry that she would bring him some McDonalds when she left the club. He was hungry as ever, so he called her to see where she was at.

London was getting hot and bothered from all the slow dancing. She was ready to go and get some from her man who had been texting her telling her to bring her ass home. Lorren on the other hand had to get home before Rico did. Lorren had asked her brother Landon to watch RJ while she went out. So Lorren was on a time schedule. Tracey was ready to go and see Keith who had asked her to spend the night with him. All the ladies had a good time at the club and planned to hook up again soon.

Chapter 13

Lorren Returns

Everybody rode with London that night except Danni. So, after London dropped the remaining of the girls off, she drove her sister to her mother's house to pick up RJ. On the ride to Lorren house, Lorren was getting impatient by the minute because she had to beat Rico's ass home. She had a nice time at the club with her girls and didn't want his bipolar ass to fuck up her night.

When London pulled in the driveway, Lorren gave her sister a hug. She picked up a sleeping RJ from the backseat and carried him into the house. Once she got in the house, everything seemed to be in the place that she left it, so she proceeded to put RJ to bed. After she put him to bed, she felt warm air on her neck.

"Where the fuck you been at Lorren?" Rico said in a raspy voice.

Lorren jumped because she wasn't expecting him to be home.

"I was at London's house." She responded scared half to death.

"You a lying bitch, Lorren, because I went passed the house. London's car wasn't there," replied Rico.

Lorren began to walk out of RJ's room and said, "I ain't gotta lie to you nigga."

He followed her into their room, telling her how he would kill her ass if he ever found out she was cheating on him.

She turned to him and said angrily, "Ain't nobody cheating on your dumb ass. You ain't gonna do shit to me nigga."

Rico stared her down and said, "Keep fucking with me and you'll see what happens."

Lorren laughed at his ass. She knew he didn't like to be laughed at, but she did it to get under his skin. He turned and walked towards the closet and pulled out a gun, aiming it at her.

With cold eyes filled with no remorse, he said, "Why do you make me act this way?"

Lorren stopped laughing and stared at him with fear in her eyes. Then she said, "What you going to do with that? What you talking about making you act like what?"

"If you ever try and leave me or cheat on me, I'm going to kill you. Every time you lie to me Lorren I just want to hurt somebody."

"So I'm the reason that you want to hurt someone?"

"Yeah, you the reason, I swear if you wasn't my baby mother I would have been killed you."

"So you saying the only reason I am alive is because I'm your baby mother."

"Yeah that's what I'm saying. But, if you ever I mean ever cheat or try and leave me; baby mother or not I would kill you." Rico said that statement forceful while still putting the gun at her.

Even though Lorren was scared, she would never let him see her sweat because if she did he would continue to pull guns out on her. After that, she knew she had to get away from him and she need to move fast.

The next day that she woke up she heard cartoons on and she knew RJ was up so she went to look for him. He was in his room watching TV and when he heard his mother walk in he turned to her and smiled and said, "Daddy told me to say call him."

"Ok honey, thank you for the message. What do you want to eat?" she asked RJ.

"I don't know mommy, I want tacos." He said laughing real hard.

"You can't have tacos now; its breakfast's time. Do you want some pancakes?"

"Yay I want pancakes." RJ said happily.

Lorren went to fix her son something to eat. She didn't want to call Rico but she knew if she didn't it would be trouble when he got home.

"Yo?" Rico said answering the phone when Lorren called him.

"You told me to call you. What's up?" Lorren asked.

"I wanted to tell you don't take your ass nowhere today." Rico said in a firm voice.

"Today is Sunday my mother is cooking dinner today and she wanted us to come over."

"I don't give a fuck. You not going and that's it."

"Look, if it was anywhere else I wouldn't go, but this is my mother's house. She wants you to come too. So I already told her we would come."

"I'll talk to you when I get home." He said before he hung up on her.

Lorren knew he was crazy so she try hard not to argue with him. After she fixed her and RJ something to eat, they watched TV together and she went to clean the kitchen and find RJ something to wear to her mother's house for dinner.

While she put RJ in the tub, she heard the front door close, right off the back Lorren knew who it was, so she focused on washing her son. Out of nowhere Rico came in the bathroom and looked at her. A cheerful RJ saw his daddy and said, "Hey daddy, are you going to grandma house too?"

Rico just looked at his son then at Lorren and said, "Yeah little man, I'm going over your grandmother house."

After she got RJ out the tub and dressed, Lorren tried her best to avoid Rico and get dressed in peace. After her success in getting dressed in peace, she told them she was ready to go to her mother's house. The three of them left the house and got in Rico's truck. The ride to Lorren's mother's house was quiet and Lorren could tell Rico didn't want to go. He didn't like going to her mother's house because he had beef with dudes around the way. When Rico started dating Lorren, he used to pick her up from her mother's house and he would always get into it with all the dudes around her way because they use to look at Lorren with pure lust. They finally made it to Lorren's mom's house and Rico already started having a staring contest with the corner boys. The only reason they didn't do anything to Rico was because he was Lorren's boyfriend and they had respect for her and her family.

"Hey ma, what you cook? It smells great." Lorren said as she made her way to the kitchen. Once they walked in the kitchen, she saw her sister, who was helping their mother Lacey.

"Hey ma, what's up London?" Lorren said as she went to give her mother and sister a kiss.

"What's up y'all?" Rico said as he gave them a hug. London wasn't really fond of Rico, neither was Lacey, but she dealt with him because he was her daughter's boyfriend and the father of her grandson.

"Nothing is up. I just felt like making dinner for my family. I don't get to see you all as much as I would like to. So I figure dinner would be a chance to see all of you." Lacey said not hiding the fact that she was excited about having all her children over for dinner.

RJ came running in the kitchen screaming, "Grandma, grandma". He loved his grandma and every time he came to her house no matter what time it is, he would scream grandma until he found her. When he found Lacey, he ran to her and jumped in her arms. He showered her with kisses and hugs. Then he went to his auntie London. He expressed the same passion to his aunt. Rico and RJ left the kitchen and went to the living room to watch ESPN where Keith was at. While the men was in the living room, the girls was cooking and talking.

"So, London, when are you going to give me some grandchildren?" Lacey asked her daughter catching everyone off of guard.

"Ma, we already talked about this. When I finish with school, then I'm going to considered children but right now Keith and I are trying to focus on our career now." London explained to her mother.

Lorren just looked at her sister because she knew what she was saying about having kids were BS. She knew her sister loved kids and wanted them ASAP. Keith didn't want any children so that caused her sister to back up on having any.

While the women were talking, Landon came in the house. He walked straight to the kitchen.

"Oh my look who is, all of my favorite women." Landon said, before he went around and gave his mother and sisters a kiss.

They just smiled at him, realizing how handsome he was growing up to be. Landon was dark skin with hazel sexy eyes; he had a perfect smile, six foot one inch tall and a sexy body. Landon got his looks from his father and eyes from his mother.

"Hey bro! You getting too grown." Lorren said to her younger brother.

"Girl I am grown." He said in response to Lorren comment.

RJ must have heard his uncle's voice because he came running out the living room. He saw his uncle and jumped on him then start to fake beating him up. Every time they saw each other, they would start play fighting. Landon would pop him upside the head and RJ would punch him in the stomach. That was their entertainment. While they were playing in the kitchen, Lacey told them to get out. Landon went in the living room where all the men were at. As soon as he walked in and saw Rico, he took a deep breath and prepared his self for the slick comments that would come out his mouth.

Rico looked up and saw Landon and said, "What's up punk? What you know about sports?"

Landon looked at this pretty boy, want-to-be and said "Fuck you Rico. I know more about sports than you."

Rico laughed at him then added, "Yo that was the gayest shit I ever heard."

"You know what, fuck you bitch." Landon said. He was heated and hated when people called him gay.

Rico just kept on laughing at him. Keith figured he would stand up for Landon.

"Yo Rico, stop messing with him." Keith said calm, because he knew Rico is a hot head.

"Alright man." Rico said.

An hour later, the women told the guys that it was time to eat. They ate dinner and everything was going great until Lorren's phone rang and she didn't answer it. Rico peeped her ignoring the call and decided to say something while they was at the table.

"Who was that Lorren?" Rico asked still stuffing his face.

"What are you talking about?" Lorren asked not really in the mood for his BS.

"Don't fucking play dumb, Lorren. I don't give a fuck if we are at your mother's table." Rico said acting crazy.

"Look you are disrespecting my mother and you need to chill. It was India calling me and if you don't believe me here is my phone." Lorren gave Rico the phone and he went to the missed calls and it was India. He felt stupid. He apologized to Lacey and everyone else at the table. After dinner Lacey was upset at the way Rico acted at the table and she wanted to talk with her daughter.

"What do you want to talk to me about, ma?" Lorren asked walking to her mother room.

"Is that boy hitting you?" Lacey asked her daughter not happy with the way Rico acted at the table.

"No ma, he never hit me, he just make's threats that he don't go through with." Lorren explained to her mother.

"Well, if he ever tries and put his hands on you don't you feel obligated to stay with him because of RJ. Leave before he hurt you baby." Lacey said showing her concern.

"I will, ma, I promise. I love you." Lorren said before giving her mother a kiss.

"Lord please protect my baby." Lacey said once her daughter left the house. She was so scared that Rico would hurt Lorren one day.

Chapter 14

Lisa's Date with the Dream Goddess

This is the day I been waiting for my whole life. Ever since I was young, I wanted to date this man. Now I am getting a chance. It is Wednesday and Darnell finally called and asked me out. I am nervous but at the same time I can't wait to see how he carries himself on a date. I wonder why he wanted to take me out on a Wednesday and not on a Saturday or Friday. I'm not going to complain. Maybe this is the only time he isn't busy. As Lisa sat on her bed getting ready for her date all kind of thoughts ran through her mind.

Lisa was completely dressed, when she heard her doorbell rang. She added some perfume and went down stairs to meet her dream God. Before she went to open the door she told Larry she would be home late and make sure he go to bed at a good time because he had school tomorrow.

When Lisa opened the door, she almost fainted from the way that Darnell looked. Darnell was dressed to kill and he looked like he just came from the barber shop, he smelled so good and his smile, OMG. Lisa had to catch herself before she fainted and made a fool of herself.

"How you doing beautiful?" Darnell said in a deep voice that made Lisa blush and say clean up on lane seven.

Lisa, being light skin, couldn't hide the fact that she was blushing so hard. "I'm doing well." She replied in a shy tone.

"Cool, let's get to this date then." He walked her to his car and opened the car door for her.

They went to Georgia Brown down town. They had a nice dinner, talking and getting to know each other better. After dinner, neither of them wanted the date to end. So Darnell drove to his condo so they could continue to talk and enjoy each other company.

"Your condo is nice. It's well decorated for a man's place." Lisa said liking her surroundings.

"Thank you, I had a decorator to come out and design the place. Would you like something to drink, Lisa?"

"Yes I'll have water." Lisa said having to keep a clear head around Darnell.

He went to the kitchen. When he returned, he had a bottle of water, two glasses, champagne, and some strawberries with melted chocolate. He poured her a glass and raised his glass to make a toast.

"I would like to toast to the start of something new." Darnell said. Lisa was falling in Darnell's trap.

Darnell knew Lisa's past and knew she was a virgin. He had everything planned. He knew he was going to bring her back to his place after dinner and he planned on fucking her tonight and not talking to her anymore.

Lisa was buying into his slick ways. She didn't even know that he was trying to get in her pants. After a few drinks and the soft music playing in the background, Lisa was real relaxed. Once Darnell realized that she was relaxed, he leaned in and kissed Lisa. She was caught off guard so she jumped back from him.

"Did I do something wrong?" Darnell asked Lisa.

"No, you just caught me off of guard." Lisa said. She loved the way his lips felt on hers. So Lisa leaned in and kissed Darnell. They kissed for a minute then he moved his hand up under her dress. When Lisa realized what he was doing, she broke the kiss.

"No, Darnell! I like you, but I'm not ready to have sex with you." Lisa said knowing that he wouldn't be happy by being rejected.

"It's ok beautiful, I just wanted to do something special for you." He said, upset because he wanted to hit it.

"Do something special how? You already took me out to eat and gave me a wonderful evening. What more can you do?" Lisa asked while showing her appreciation.

"Well, I can start by doing this." Darnell said as he kissed her neck then slowly massaging it with his tongue. "Then I was going to do this." He said while putting his hand under her dress and massaging her clit. Then he stopped licking her neck and pulled her panties off and lowered his head under her dress. Lisa was being eaten out for the first time in her life. She didn't know what to expect, but she liked everything that he was doing to her. When she came her legs began to shake and she came all over his face.

"Damn baby you taste good." Darnell said when he came up for air.

Lisa was nervous and didn't know what to say so she just smiled at him, while trying to catch her breath. Out of nowhere, Darnell pulled his dick out of his pants and said, "I did you so now are you going to do me or are you going to give me some pussy?"

Lisa never saw this side of Darnell and she was scared, so she didn't want to upset him and she wanted to leave so she said, "Are you joking? Because I didn't ask you to do anything for me and I don't plan on losing my virginity on the first date." Lisa stated seriously.

Darnell looked at her and laughed while putting his dick back in his pants. "I'm joking with you baby. Are you ready to go home?"

"Yes it's getting late and I have to work tomorrow." Lisa said ready to get out of his condo and home where she felt safe.

"Ok, let's go baby." Darnell took Lisa home and before she got out the car he looked at her and said one day we would finish what we started. Lisa smiled even though she was thinking *'I don't think so.'*

Later that night....

The date was getting to Lisa and she needed to talk to someone and she needed to talk to someone fast. She decided to call her cousin, Rachel. Rachel was raised by their great grandmother too, so she and Lisa were close like sisters. Lisa also knew that Rachel is always up and she always gave her advice about boys because she was a year older than Lisa.

It was 3:00a.m. And she was calling Rachel and hoping that she is still up.

"Hello." Rachel said sounding wide awake at 3:00 in the morning.

"Hey Rachel, I need your advice." Lisa said.

"Hey Lisa Boo, what's going on with my little cousin?"

"Well, I had a date with Darnell tonight. You know Darnell, the pastor son." Lisa said making sure she knew who she was talking about.

"Yeah I know who he is. The want-to-be player." Rachel said not liking the fact that her cousin went out with him and mostly he would try and play her.

"Well, we went out tonight. The evening started great, but then he invited me back to his condo, where we talked and drank some champagne. Everything was going great till he kissed me. The kiss was great, but he was moving his hand up my dress." Lisa didn't even get a chance to finish the story before Rachel interrupted her.

"Did that son of a bitch rape you? Please Lisa let me know if he hurt you. If he hurt you I promise, I would kill his ass while he faking like he is Mr. goodie good."

"Calm down Rachel, I wasn't raped and no I didn't have sex with him. He went down on me and after he did I felt so bad and when he was done he pulled his pants down and told me to suck him off or give him some pussy because he ate me out." Once again Lisa was interrupted by Rachel.

"What? Is that mother fucker asking to get dealt with?" Rachel was getting madder and madder by the minute.

"I always liked him and wanted him to be my first, but now I see that he is an asshole."

"Yes honey, I'm glad you see him for what he really is, a user."

"So what do I do when he calls me?"

74

"Tell him you don't want to be around him because you didn't feel safe." Rachel explained still wanting to kick his ass.

"I still have to see him every Sunday, Rachel." Lisa didn't want to tell her cousin that she still liked him. She knew her cousin. She would go off on her.

"I know that Lisa, but I know you, Lisa, you won't say anything to him and he is going to think that it was fine to pull his dick out and tell you to suck it or give him some pussy." Rachel was getting heated at her cousin because sometimes she doesn't have any backbone and was so naive.

"Thank you Rachel for your advice. I'll see you Friday, at Uncle Rick house." Lisa said.

"Ok honey, be safe and I love you, Lisa."

"I love you too, Rachel."

Chapter 15

India

It was Thursday and it was time to party. India was going out with her cousin Peaches who was a hood bunny and a stripper. India and Peaches grew up together. Unlike India, Peaches was born and raised in the ghetto. Even though they were raised differently, they were close and every chance they got they went out.

"What club we going to tonight?" India asked while she put on her freak dress.

"Girl, we going to the club where all the ballers are at, Club Diamonds." Peaches said hyped to trick some ballers.

India and Peaches were dressed to kill. They walked to the front of the line and were let in without paying or having to wait in line.

"Girl, do you see all these ballers in her tonight?" Peaches said excited, ready to get her Mack on.

"Yes, let go to the bar. I need a drink." India said.

They made their way to the bar and as soon as they stepped up there, a player asked to buy their drinks. After they received their drinks, they hit the dance floor. They were dancing with all dudes, getting numbers left and right. After they were tired of dancing, they went back to the bar to have a seat and drink. While they were there, India looked in the mirror over the bar and noticed him right away.

"Damn." India said out loud.

"What's wrong with you, girl?" Peaches wanted to know.

"I think that nigga got a tracker or something on me. Everywhere I go here he is."

"Who are you talking about?"

"Do you see that sexy, brown skin nigga to your right?" India said.

"There are two of them. Which one?"

"The one with the dreads locks."

"Oh he is sexy. That's your man?" Peaches asked.

"No, but he is trying to be, hard." India said but couldn't keep her eyes off of Kevin. Kevin was brown skin with dread locks, with a nice body, and he had the shadow going on. He had on a fly ass outfit that screamed out "I got money."

"Girl, he looks paid. You need to go get that." Peaches said showing her gold digger side.

"If I want him, I can have him." India said confident.

India kept a close eye on Kevin as he moved around the club and watched the bitches flock all over him. India was busy drinking and talking to this dude from Baltimore. She didn't want to talk to him because he was a bamma, but he brought her and Peaches a drink. While they were talking, she never noticed Kevin walking up to her.

"Hey beautiful, who is this bamma nigga you talking too?" Kevin asked looking the dude up and down. Kevin had three dudes with him.

"This is my friend, James. How did you know I was here?" India asked curious to know how he found out she was there.

"I peeped you when you walked in and I saw you playing these lame ass niggas." Kevin said. "Yo my nigga you got to go, her man is over here to buy her drinks now." Kevin said to James from B-More.

India didn't say anything just let Kevin take control of the situation. He grabbed her hand and led her and Peaches to VIP. Once they got to VIP, they had drinks left and right. India noticed Shawn sitting in VIP drinking. So she walked over to him.

"Hey Shawn, why are you in the club and my friend is at home pregnant with your child?" India said serious.

Shawn looked up at India and smiled. "Ms. India, I'm working so I can take care of your friend and my child. By the way after I finish this drink, I'm going home to her."

"Well, so you can know I'm about to call her now and tell her where you at." India said while pulling out her phone.

Shawn laughed at her and handed her his phone. "She already beat you to the chase. She just told me to get out the club and bring my ass home. So, that is where I'm heading once I leave here."

"Ok. I'm still calling her." India said making sure he wasn't playing her friend.

She walked over where Peaches was sitting talking to a group of guys.

"Who was that fine ass nigga you was just talking to?" Peaches asked her cousin once she came over to the table.

"Who Shawn?" India asked not sure who Peaches was talking about.

"I guess that's his name."

"Oh, that's just Kim's baby daddy."

"What! Kim is pregnant?" Peaches asked shocked.

"Yeah, my girl is two months and so fucking emotional."

"Damn, I thought that stuck up bitch would never ruin her body for a baby."

"Yeah she thought the same thing." India said.

While they drank some more, Shawn got up and walked over to India.

"Alright sis, I'm about to go home and take care of the cry baby."

"Don't talk about my girl like that. I'm going to make sure I tell her too." She said before giving him a hug.

After Shawn left, Kevin talked to Shawn for a minute then made his way to India who was surrounded by dudes.

"Yo you are going home with me?" Kevin asked India.

India just looked at him and replied, "Naw, I'm going home. I have school and work tomorrow so I'm going to pass."

"I can take you to school and where ever else you need to go." Kevin said, really wanting her to come home with him.

"No thank you, Kevin, I'm about to leave." She said as she got up and grabbed Peaches arm telling her it was time to go.

"Girl, I'm not ready to go yet. Why are you in a hurry?" Peaches asked because normally she was the one dragging India out of the club.

"Can we just leave?" India asked ready to go because she could tell Kevin was catching feelings and she didn't want to fall for him.

While India was trying to get Peaches to leave, she started to think about a promise she made. India made a promise to herself when she was in high school to never fall for another guy as she did with Chris. Chris was India's first and she was so in love with him. He was the best thing that ever happened to her. Then out of nowhere Chris told her he didn't want to be with her no more. India was so heartbroken that she cried for months and became so depressed. So after Chris, India promised herself to never fall for another man. If it was anything, they would fall for her and she would leave them.

"Ok. I'm ready India. You want to leave when the ballers starting to show a girl some love?" Peaches said upset.

She gave Kevin a peck on the cheek and her and Peaches left the club. As they rode to India's house, she couldn't shake Kevin out of her mind. "Come on India, you can't fall for no nigga you remember how Chris treated you when you let him get close." India said to herself.

Chapter 16

Kim

It was a long day and all Kim wanted to do is get in the bed and take the longest nap in the world. As Kim put on some sweat pants and climbed in the bed, Shawn walked in the room. Kim tried to put her head under the covers but that didn't work because all he did was pull them off her head and start talking.

"Hey cry baby. How was your day?" He asked as he kissed her on the forehead.

"It was cool, I'm just tired. This baby is making me tired by the minute." Kim said trying to send hints to him.

"Oh is that a clue that you want to go to sleep?" Shawn asked even though he knew the answer.

"Yes. And don't think I didn't know you called me a cry baby last night at the club." She said letting him know that she talked to India.

"You are a cry baby. But you my cry baby." He said before his phone rang.

"Hello." Shawn said, while Kim put the covers back over her head to try and fall back to sleep. It was hard for Kim to go to sleep because Shawn was talking loud. She just laid there with her head under the covers listening to his conversation.

"So you are feeling Shorty?" Shawn asked the caller, who Kim took to the conclusion that it was Kevin.

"You know Shorty have reputation for being a hoe."

"Well, I feel if you like that girl that much then go for it. She is right here trying to go to sleep, but I won't let her go to sleep." Shawn said to the caller.

"Babe, Kevin said hey." Shawn said to Kim while pulling the covers from over her head.

"Hi Kevin." Kim said.

After Shawn got off the phone with Kevin, he got under the covers with Kim who had dosed off. While she was sleeping, he just stared at her. He did that every time she slept. He loved Kim so much but he knew loving her so much would hurt her one day. So he got out the bed and went downstairs to do business while Kim slept.

About an hour into her nap, her house phone began to ring and ring. She wasn't going to answer, but she knew it was a family member. She wanted Shawn to answer the phone, but he was in the basement and he didn't add a phone down there.

"Hello." Kim said half sleep.

"Baby girl, I know you are not sleep." She knew off the back who that was calling. It was Malik her brother. No matter how old she got he still called her Baby girl.

"Hey Malik, yes I was sleep. I am kind of tired." Kim said not trying to let her brother know that she is pregnant, because he acted like he was her daddy.

"Well get your ass up because I'm on my way to pick you up. Me, you and Angel is going out. I need to spend some time with the women in my life." Malik was the type of brother who took very good care of his sisters as if they were his children.

"Malik, I'm not really in the mood today to go out." Kim said.

"Look baby girl, you bringing your ass and that's it." Malik said in a firm voice. When he said something, everyone knew not to go against his view.

"Ok, what time are you coming to get me?" Kim asked not really in the mood.

"I would be there in an hour." Malik said before hanging up.

Kim got out the bed and decided to put her clothes back on. After she did that, she walked to the basement to see what Shawn was doing. When she went to the basement, Shawn was knocked out on the couch with the TV on ESPN. Since he didn't let her take a nap, she figured he wouldn't get one either. So she opened his eye lids and he jumped up.

"What the hell you doing Kim?" Shawn asked mad cause his nap was getting good.

"Oh nothing I figured if I can't sleep then you can't." Kim said flopping on the couch next to him.

"Why you can't sleep?"

"Malik is on his way to get me. I'm nervous telling him that I'm pregnant." Kim said.

"Kim, I respect the fact that your brother was like your father and took care of you and your sister, but he is your brother not your father and you are a grown woman. It's your life." Shawn said knowing that Kim looked up to her brother and knows his approval is everything to her.

An hour later, the house phone was ringing again. This time Shawn answered the phone while Kim went to put her shoes on.

"Kim, Malik is outside." Shawn said as he got off the phone with Malik.

Kim came down stairs and gave Shawn a kiss. "I'm going to be working tonight by the time you get back so call me and let me know you made it back in the house. I love you, ma." Shawn said before she left the house.

"Ok. I love you too." Kim said.

She walked up to her brother's truck and got in the back because their little sister Angel was in the front. Kim was glad that Angel was in the front because she didn't want to be close to Malik. He can sense when something is wrong with his sisters. They pulled up at Outback steak house restaurant. They were seated immediately.

"What would you have to drink today?" The waitress asked.

Malik always ordered for them every time they went out. "I would have some goose straight up, she would have a fruit punch and she would have an apple martini." He said giving their drink orders.

"I would have a fruit punch as well; I don't want the apple martini." Kim said.

When the waiter walked off, Malik looked at his sister weird. Every time they went out to eat she got an Apple martini; now she didn't want one. "When you start not wanting an Apple martini with your meal, Kim?"

"I haven't been in the mood to drink, Malik." Kim said not ready to tell her brother that she was pregnant.

"Well if she don't want one I want one." Angel said trying to see if her brother or sister would buy her one.

Malik and Kim looked at her. Malik said, "Angel pies don't play like that."

The waitress brought the drinks back and then they ordered. They sat and talked about school and everything. Kim was happy because that would buy her sometime to figure out a way to tell Malik that she was pregnant. Kim ate all her food and she was craving ice cream with caramel, so she ordered it. While Kim ate her food, Malik and Angel just looked at her. Kim was the one who never finished her meal and she always ate healthy because she worked out a lot.

"Baby girl, are you ok?" Malik asked after he saw her kill the ice cream sundae.

"Yeah I'm fine. Why you ask that?" Kim said even though she knew why he asked.

"He asked caused you just killed that damn ice cream." Angel said.

"Watch your mouth Angel pies." Malik said.

"My bad but that's what she did to that ice cream and her food."

"Baby girl, what is going on and don't you say nothing because I know you better than you know yourself." Malik said.

Kim knew it was time to let him know, she knew she was going to have to tell him sooner or later. So Kim took a deep breath and said, "I'm pregnant."

Malik was silent for a minute. Then he looked at Kim. She could see the disappointment deep in his eyes. "So you are pregnant, Kim?" She could tell he was mad because he didn't call her baby girl.

"Yes." Kim said nervous, not sure what he was going to say.

"How many months are you?"

"I'm two months." Kim answered each question nervous.

"What the fuck were you thinking, Kim? You are not done with dental school, and you talking about having a baby." Malik started raising his voice, showing his anger because he knew his sister wasn't ready for a baby.

Kim was on the verge of crying because her brother was showing the fact that he didn't approve of him.

"I can take care of the baby. I have a job and have a man that is going to take care of the baby." Kim said to Malik.

"Fuck that. You can't take care of a motherfucking baby. You need to focus on school. How the fuck do you know that punk ass nigga going to take care of that motherfucking baby? How you know he going to take care of his because he told you he was going to take care of you and the baby. Man, fuck that you getting an abortion." Malik said getting pissed off by the minute. Kim started to cry now and she was really hurting.

While Kim was crying, Angel tried to help her, but Malik got the waitress' attention so he could pay the bill. When Malik paid the bill, he told his sisters to come on. When they got back in the truck, no one would say anything. They drove to their mother's house in complete silence. When they got to the house which they grew up in, they went in to see their mother. When they walked in the house the only person who spoke to their mother was Angel. She spoke to her then went to her room to get on the phone.

"So, what went on at this dinner that has my two oldest children not speaking to their mother?" Mia asked wanting to know what had them not talking.

Malik took a deep breath to hide his anger from his mother. "Hey ma, that dumb ass daughter of yours is pregnant."

"Who the fuck are you calling dumb?" Kim asked getting angry at Malik.

"I'm talking to your dumb ass. Sitting here listening to a man talking about he is going to take care of you and a baby. That's some bullshit." Malik yelled at Kim.

Mia had enough of the yelling that was going on so she said something, "Both of y'all be quiet. Kim are you pregnant?"

Kim looked at her mother and said, "Yes, I'm two months."

"She ain't going to be pregnant for long because tomorrow I'm taking her ass to get an abortion." Malik said.

"Fuck you Malik; I'm not getting anybody's fucking abortion." Kim yelled back to Malik.

"Shut the fuck up both of y'all. Kim calm down, and Malik be quite this is not your life." Mia was getting upset because her children were acting crazy.

"Kim, do you want to have this baby?" Mia asked.

"Yes, I want to have my baby. I know Shawn will be there for me and my baby." Kim said.

"Well, if you want the child, then you live your life." Mia said.

Malik looked at his mother like she was crazy. "Ma, do you think it is best for your daughter who has one more year to complete dental school to stop her career to have a child?" Malik asked a little calmer.

"I feel it's her life and she can live it the way she wants to."

"Well, I'm her brother and I want her to think about what she is doing to her career." Malik said.

"I have thought about it and I want to have my child and if you don't like it then that's on you. I appreciate everything you did for me, but I'm grown Malik. I am a grown woman who can take care of herself."

"Well, where is your baby daddy? I need to talk to him." Malik asked. Kim was happy to call Shawn because Malik was moving a step closer to accepting her pregnancy.

Kim called Shawn who was out in the streets hustling.

"Hey ma. You home?" Shawn asked as soon as he answered the phone.

"No I'm at my mother's house. I need you to come pass here." Kim informed him.

"Ok ma, I'm on my way." Shawn got in his car and left.

An hour later Shawn pulled up in front of Kim mother's house. He knocked on the door and Angel let him in. When Shawn walked in he gave Angel a hug and followed her into the living room where the rest of the family was sitting. Shawn spoke to everyone while giving Mia and Kim a kiss and giving Malik a pound.

He looked at Kim who looked as if she had been crying "Are you ok, ma?" Shawn asked concerned.

"Yeah, I'm fine" Kim replied.

"So how do you plan on taking care of my sister and this baby that she is carrying?" Malik asked getting right to the point.

"I have money and I love your sister so she will be fine." Shawn said catching Malik's drift.

"Well, I'm going to tell you like this, if you ever and I mean ever, hurt my sister I will kill your ass." Malik said.

Kim looked at Malik with a smile because she knew that meant he was accepting the fact that she was pregnant. Kim jumped out of her seat and onto her brother, hugging him tight. When his sisters are happy, he is happy. He still had a feeling that Shawn was going to do Kim wrong, so he wanted to protect her and that is what his mission would be while she was pregnant.

Shawn stayed around for a little while longer, then he told Kim he was going back to hit the streets. After he left, Kim had a good time with her family. Then around ten that night,

Malik took Kim home and promised her that he would pick her up from school to take her to lunch because they had to talk.

Chapter 17

Danni

Danni wanted to know why her father asked her to come over his house for dinner. Danni haven't been to her father's house since her freshman year at college. Now out of the blue, he called her and told her he was having dinner at his house and wanted her to come.

"Bryon, my dad want me to have dinner with him tonight." Danni informed him because she didn't want any problems with him about her whereabouts.

"Ok, that's fine baby. Just make sure you fix me something to eat before you leave this house though." Bryon said not caring if she went to her father house.

"What would you like to eat tonight?" Danni was trying to be very nice and ask questions because she didn't want an ass whooping, like the one she received two days ago.

Bryon beat the shit out of Danni because the guy Moe she met at Club Passion called her phone. When Moe called, Danni had forgotten that she gave him her number because she was so drunk that night. She had gotten in the shower and her phone rang. Bryon answered it and when he heard Moe's voice he went off. He went after Danni who was in the shower and didn't know what was going on. He beat the shit out of her in the shower. After that Danni tried her best to stay out of his way.

"Fix me some steak and potatoes." Bryon said.

Danni went in the kitchen and made his dinner. After an hour, his dinner was ready and she fixed his plate and went to clean up the kitchen. After he ate and the house was clean, she got in her car and drove to her father's house. When she pulled up she saw her sister Staci's car and knew this was a family outing.

Danni parked and walked up to her father's big ass house, and rang the doorbell. This cute little boy who looked like he was ten years old answered the door. Danni not thinking spoke and walked into the house.

"Hey dad." Danni spoke when she saw her father and gave him a hug.

"Hey sweetheart. How are you? You looking more and more like me every day." Danny said to his daughter. He always praised Danni because she looked like him, that's why he name her Danielle and nicknamed her after him.

"I'm doing fair daddy. What's the deal with the dinner?" Danni asked. Before Danny could respond, Staci walked out of the bathroom and said hey to her sister.

"I just wanted to spend time with my children. I haven't seen my babies in a long time." Danny said not letting them know who the little boy was.

Danni accepted her father's response and went to the living room where the little boy and Staci sat watching TV, while their father was cooking on the grill. An hour later, Danny was done cooking and they all went to the table to eat.

Danny looked around the table looking at his daughter who grew up to be very beautiful women even though he put them through a lot when they were growing up.

"So Danni, how is school going?" Danny asked.

"It's going ok. I can't complain." She said to answer her father's question.

"Staci, how is school going?" Danny asked his other daughter.

"It's ok. I'm tired of it." Staci said.

"Dad, who is little man?" Danni asked wanting to know who the little boy was.

"One of the reasons for this dinner was for me to let the both of y'all meet your little brother Daniel." Danny said informing the girls they had a little brother.

Both girls looked at their father and said "What!!!!"

Danny looked at them and then at Daniel, who just sat there already knowing who the both of them where.

"Danielle and Staci this is your brother, Daniel. Daniel these are your sisters." Danny introduced them.

"How old are you Daniel?" Danni asked her little brother.

"I'm ten years old." Daniel said.

Staci, always being the outspoken one, looked at her father and said "Why the fuck you ain't tell us that we have a little brother. You hid this from us for ten years. What kind of fucking father are you?"

"Watch your damn mouth in my house, Staci. I was going to tell the both of you but I never knew how to tell you. I don't need to explain myself to neither of you. I'm the damn father." Danny said.

"You hid that you had a son for ten years now you telling me to watch my mouth. You know what dad fuck you. You ain't been shit to me. I don't even know why I came over. You been a shitty ass father and you still are." Staci said to her father.

Danni being a daddy's girl didn't want her sister and father to get into it, so she interrupted Staci before she could continue. "Staci, shut up. He is still your father whether you like it or not. He may have hid that we have a brother but he still is our father and you need to show him some respect."

Staci looked at her sister as if she was crazy and said, "Respect, Respect!! It's because of him that we are fucked up. Rather you want to hide it or not Danielle. It's not that he hid we have a brother, he did some fucked up shit when we was younger and now you sitting here talking about show this ass hole some respect."

Staci was mad because her sister was acting like their father never did anything to make their life a living hell. Staci felt that Danielle should be madder because their father was married to her mother.

"You can leave, Staci. You're just like your mother anyway, a drug addicted, selfish bitch." Danny was so pissed off because of the way his daughter was acting that he called her a bitch and told her secret. He knew his daughter was on drugs because she went to the bathroom often and when she came out her eyes were glossy. She reminded him so much of his self as a hot head who didn't give a fuck about no one but his self.

"I'm not going anywhere and you right I am just like my mother. I would rather be like her then like you, you son of bitch. Drug addicted! You got some nerve saying some shit like that. I was there when you and my mother was doing drugs right in front of me. So if you ask me I am just like you. A selfish, spoiled, drug addicted, ass hole." Staci looked her father dead in the eyes and left it just like that.

Danielle didn't like the atmosphere right then. She told Daniel to come out to the living room so they could get to know each other, while Staci and Danny could get over their differences and work out their daughter/father relationship.

Danielle looked at Daniel closely and she saw a lot of features that they got from their father.

"So Daniel what do you like to do?" Danni asked.

"I like to play video games and play football." He responded shyly.

"How long have you been living with our father?"

"My mom died when I was nine and my mom told my auntie to take me to my father. I just found out about him. So this is new to me." Daniel said letting Danni know that he just met his father.

"Oh wow. Do you need anything?" Danni asked knowing it was hard for him to move with a father he just met.

"No, I am fine. Danni sometimes I need someone to talk to. Can I call you when I need someone to talk too?"

"Sure you can. I would like that. How about we go out once a week?" Danni said making a connection with her brother.

Daniel smiled and agreed.

Danni stayed at her father's house for another hour. Then she decided to go home and get some rest so she can get ready for work and school.

Chapter 18

Tracey

Tracey woke up early on a Friday because she was going to visit Zoe. She wanted to break it off with him but she didn't want to make it seem as if she was leaving him hanging. After getting ready and making sure she had on proper clothes for the visit, she left out her house.

Once she made her way to the prison, she filled out the papers and went through all the security. She sat at the table waiting for Zoe to come out. When she looked up and saw a six foot four inches tall, brown skin dude, with a muscular body, and long shoulder length dreads, all she could do was smile. He was so sexy and she loved her some Zoe.

When he saw her, he smiled and walked over to her and kissed and hugged her for a while.

"Hey baby. I'm glad you came to see a nigga." Zoe said to Tracey.

"Yeah I had to come see my baby." She replied.

"So why don't you have on a skirt?" Zoe asked Tracey.

"Because I came here to talk to you, not have sex." She responded.

"We can talk on the phone. When you come and visit me I want some pussy." Zoe stated.

"Well, I'm not feeling this relationship anymore, Zoe."

"What?"

"I can't do the time anymore with you. I love you, believe me I do, but I need you by my side, I need you to be there for me." Tracey stated.

"If you loved me, you won't be on the verge of leaving me. I fucked up so now you leaving me. It must be another nigga that got your mother fucking attention." Zoe said angry.

"No it's not another guy. I'm just getting tired of doing the time. I feel like I'm on lock down. I love you but I have to do me. I will continue to be your friend and visit you and everything." Tracey said before getting up to leave. She cut her visit short and left to go and meet up with her brothers and father.

On the way to Tracey's father's house, she kept thinking about Zoe and wondering if she was making the right decision. "Oh well, it's already done." She said to herself.

Once she reached her father's house, she got ready for her brothers. They raised her to be a hard ass. No matter how old she got, they would ruff her up. When she walked in the house, she heard all of the men in the living room watching some sports, so she walked in there to see what was going on.

When she walked in the living room, her father noticed her and said, "Hey honey."

She smiled and walked over to her father and gave him a hug. "Hey daddy. What is all of the noise for?"

"Those fools betting on the fight that comes on this weekend. Are you coming over to watch it? We might have a fight party." Troy said.

While Tracey and her father talked, her brother TJ, who was the oldest came over to her and picked her up. He picked her up like she was a little baby. TJ and Tracey were the closest and Ty and Tone were closer. Ty and Tone would abuse Tracey when she was younger. Tracey stabbed Tone before when they were younger because he put a pillow case over her head and locked her in the closet. Once she got out of the closet she went to the kitchen and stabbed him in the shoulder.

"Hey TJ. Can you put me down?" Tracey asked.

"Oh my bad baby sis. You don't come around that much anymore." TJ said as he put Tracey down.

"Yeah I have been busy." She said as she saw her other brothers getting up to come and mess with her.

They walked up to her and put her in a head lock.

"Hey big head you not speaking." Tone asked while he had her in a head lock.

"I was but you ain't give me time you asshole." Tracey said.

"Where the fuck you been at? You don't fuck with your family anymore?" Ty asked.

"Get the fuck off of me Tone with your bitch ass and I been busy." Tracey said.

Tone let her go and gave her a hug. Then Ty hugged her. They might fuck her up but they are very protective of her. They all were chilling and out of nowhere there was a loud bang on the door. Troy got up to see what the commotion was about.

"Tone, that crazy girlfriend of yours is out here for you." Troy yelled to his son.

Tone got up to see what the girl wanted. "What do you want Ashley? I told you to stop talking to me, it's over."

"Nigga, it's not over until I say it's over." Ashley said. Then she reached and slapped the shit out of Tone.

"Bitch, I know you did not just slap me. I'm about to kill your ass." Tone said as he walked towards her. Before he could get to her, Ty came out and got him before he could do any damage.

"Let me go Ty, I'm going to kill this hoe. She lost her damn mind slapping me." Tone yelled, trying to break loose.

"You ain't going to kill no one, you punk ass nigga." Ashley was talking mad shit to Tone while Ty and TJ held him back.

Tracey came out the house, tired of the girl talking shit to her brother.

"Yo, Tone who is this bitch?" Tracey asked her brother.

"Some crazy hoe that doesn't understand it's over." Tone said.

Tracey didn't ask any more questions as she walked over to Ashley and punched the shit out of her. When she punched Ashley, she fell to the ground hard. Ashley tried to get up but when she attempted to get up Tracey kicked her in the stomach. Then she stomped on her face while blood came from her mouth and her eye began to turn black. She kept on repeating, "Don't you ever fuck with my brother," while she whopped her ass. When it looked like Tracey almost beat the girl to death, her father came out of the house and picked her up and took her in the house.

She chilled with her brothers and father for a little while longer then she left to go meet up with Kenny. She wanted to let Kenny know that he was the only one now.

Chapter 19

Lisa

Even though Lisa and her mother didn't have a good past, she didn't want her brother Larry to show any hatred towards her. At least once a month, she would take Larry to visit their mother. It just so happened that today was the day that they were supposed to go see their mother. Lisa knew that her mother was probably high. When they pulled up in front of the projects that they lived in before they moved with their grandmother, it brought back bad memories for Lisa. They walked up the pissy smelling hallway and made their way to apartment 310. They knocked on the door.

"Who is it?" Tonya asked through the closed door.

"It's us." Larry said informing his mother that it was him and Lisa.

Tonya opened the door recognizing her son's voice. When she opened the door, Lisa was ashamed to look at her mother. Drugs had ruined her once beautiful features and her beautiful white teeth was now yellow and looked as if they were all about to fall out.

"Oh my goodness it's my children. Come and give your mother a hug." Larry gave his mother a hug happy to see her, while Lisa just looked at her.

"How is my baby boy doing?" Tonya asked looking Larry up and down.

"I'm good, ma. I just been busy with school and basketball, other than that I been good." Larry said trying to fill his mother in on how he was doing.

"How is my Lisa doing?" She asked.

"I'm doing well Tonya." Lisa said not calling her ma.

"What's up with you calling me Tonya?" She wanted to know.

"Because, that is your name." Lisa responded back. Lisa never got smart with her mother. When she used to visit, she just didn't say anything. Now she was tired of seeing her mother look like that and wanted her to clean it up for her brothers' sake.

"I know what my name is got dammit. I'm your fucking mother show me some fucking respect." Tonya said demanding respect.

"Show some respect? You walking around her looking like a human crack pipe and you talking about show some respect. You might have birthed me but you are not my mother. My mother is dead. You was never around, all you worried about was sucking on that pipe and sucking on dick. So all I have to say to you is fuck you Tonya." Lisa said then walked out the house.

Lisa went to her car and cried her eyes out because it hurt her to talk to her mother that way, but it hurt her more to see her mother in that state of mind and looking that way. While she was crying, her cell phone rang.

"Hello." Lisa said trying not to sound like she was crying.

"Can I speak to Lisa?" a very sexy voice came through the phone that Lisa didn't recognize the voice.

"This is she, and who is calling?" Lisa asked.

"Hey beautiful this is Terence. I met you at Club Passion; you was with your girls." He said making sure she remembered him.

"Oh yeah I remembered you. I thought you would never call." She stated because she had forgot that she gave her number out at the club but as soon as he said his name, his face popped up in her head.

"I have been a little busy. So I figure I would call you when the business is steady and I can take you out."

"I understand because I've been a little busy myself."

"Why do you sound sad, beautiful?" Terence asked hearing sadness in her voice.

"I just got into it with the woman that birthed me." Lisa said not giving Tonya the title of her mother.

"Well do you want to talk about it? Matter of fact, I want to take you out for lunch."

"I'm in the middle of something." Lisa said.

"Meet me at Legal Seafood over the bridge in an hour. You do eat seafood right?" Terence asked not letting Lisa get from out of the lunch date that easily.

"Yes I do eat seafood, and I'm not sure if I can meet up with you today." Lisa said really wanting to go but didn't know why he wanted to meet up with her.

"Come on beautiful, you said you having a bad day. Maybe I can help you with that little issue. I'm a great listener and I would love your company over lunch." Terence said really feeling her style and loving the chase she was putting up.

"I guess lunch wouldn't hurt. Ok I'll see you in an hour." Lisa said before hanging up.

Lisa got herself together and went back into her mother's house. When she got in there, she informed Larry that he can hang out with their mother all day and she would come back later on and pick him up. Larry liked it around his mother's way because he had a lot of friends around there and he didn't mind staying around there for a while.

Lisa left her mother's house and went to her house. She wanted to get herself together before she had to meet Terence. When the hour passed, she was in front of Legal Seafood. When she parked her car and walked to the entrance of the restaurant she looked around for Terence but didn't see him anywhere.

"Another late ass nigga." Lisa said to herself as she waited for Terence. The whole time Lisa stood outside waiting for Terence, he was in the restaurant looking at her. So he figured that he would go out there and greet her.

"Hey beautiful, our table is ready." Terence said.

"How long have you been here?" Lisa asked after they were seated.

"I got here a few minutes before you showed up." Terence informed her.

"Oh so you saw me looking around for you?" Lisa asked.

Terence laughed and said, "Yeah. But I like that about you."

Lisa looked at him with a curious look and said, "You like the way I look around looking lost?"

Once again he laughed and said, "Naw silly. I like that you are on time. I don't like when women are late and I be waiting around for almost an hour for them."

Lisa smile and said, "Oh ok."

They walked in the restaurant and took their seat as if they were a couple for years. They ordered their drinks and food. While they waited for their food it gave them a chance to know each other better.

"So Terence, what do you do for a living?" Lisa asked wondering what kind of business he does.

"I own a few businesses." Terence said.

Then Terence looked at her and asked, "What the deal with you and your moms?"

"What you mean?" Lisa asked.

"When I called you earlier, you told me that you got into it with your moms and I told you I was a good listener." Terence said to Lisa

"Well, I was raised by my grandmother because my mother was a trick and a drug addict. So today when I took my brother over to visit my mother, she looked so bad and she tried to make me show some respect to her. I had to let her know what was on my mind." Lisa told him what was going on with her and her mom.

"So how old is your brother?" Terence asked, sensing a strong bond between her and her brother.

"He is sixteen about to turn seventeen next month." Lisa always shined when she talked about her brother.

"Oh so he not a little youngin, he is basically a grown man. I can tell you really love him." Terence said.

"He not grown, even though he thinks he is." Lisa said thinking about her brother.

"How close are you and your brother?"

"We are very close. I adopted him after my grandmother passed. So we are very close." Lisa told him the story about her growing up and how her life was when she was younger.

"Damn Shorty. You went through a lot. I guess that's why I came into your life." Terence said.

"Why do you think you came in my life?" Lisa asked wanting to know where his head was at.

"I feel I was brought into your life to help you with all the things you go through like raising a teen on your own, making sure your mother get off of drugs, and give you some happiness that you seem to lack." Terence read Lisa like a book that it scared her.

They talked for a little while longer. Then Lisa realized that it was getting late and she had to go and pick Larry up. She thanked Terence for the wonderful lunch and he promised to call her that night.

Chapter 20

India

"What's up people?" India yelled as she walked into her parent's house.

"Girl, do you have to make all that noise when you walk in the house?" India's mother said from the kitchen when she heard her daughter voice.

India walked into the kitchen and gave her mother a kiss. Then her father came into the kitchen.

"I knew I heard my princess' voice." He said once he saw his daughter and gave her a big hug and kiss on the cheek.

"Hey daddy." India said.

"Are you ok princess? Do you need anything?" India's father asked, spoiling her like he always does.

"No, daddy I'm fine. I just wanted to see my family." India said.

They all were sitting around the table and talking and catching up. Then they heard the front door open.

"Yo, where is everybody at?" Jonathan asked when he walked in the house. Jonathan was India's older brother.

"We in here, boy." Their father said.

Jonathan walked in with two of his friends. They greeted everybody.

"Y'all this is Mike and Troy. Mike and Troy, this is my sister India, my mom, and dad." Jonathan introduced his friend's to his family.

Everyone greeted each other. Then the boys went straight into the living room to watch the game, right behind them was India. As soon as she entered the living room Mike kept on looking at her. India already had in her mind that she was going to get with him tonight. It had been a week since India got some, and she wanted some from him ASAP.

"Hey Mike." India said once she sat next to him.

"What's up India?" Mike asked giving her the eye letting her know he wanted her too.

"It's all about you. I'm trying to see what's up with you?" India said.

"It's whatever and wherever." Mike said ready to do the thing anywhere.

Jonathan looked over at his sister and his friend and said, "Yo what y'all two talking about?"

"Nothing." India said. She knew how her brother was when it came to her messing with his friends.

India got up and walked up stairs to her old room signaling Mike to come with her. Once she went to her room and she got ready for Mike, he faked like he was on an important call and told Jonathan and Troy that he was going to take the call outside.

"What took you so long?" India asked Mike once he entered her room.

"I had to think of something, so I can get up here." Mike said.

"Alright enough of this talking shit, let's fuck." India said.

Mike dropped his pants, put on a condom that India handed him, and walked over to India. He roughly ripped off her clothes. He bent India over her bed and entered her from behind. Once he entered her from behind, India didn't feel nothing. She wanted to laugh because Mike had talked like he had a big dick. So she changed the position with the quickness. She got on top to ride and she was working him so much that the nigga came quick as shit. India was so disappointed that she just got up and didn't say anything to him and walked in the bathroom to wash up. Mike thought he had did something, but a chick like India would let his ass know.

When India walked back down stairs, Mike was all smiling in her face.

"Why are you smiling so hard?" India asked wanting to know.

"You know why, baby. I put it on you, didn't I?" Mike said really thinking he did something.

"First of all, I am not your baby. Second, you didn't put it on nobody." India said. She never had a problem letting a nigga know if he put it on her or if they were some shit.

"Whatever, you just don't want to admit it." Mike said.

"Naw player, I don't have a problem letting a nigga now if he was good or some shit. So, I'm letting you know you were some shit, and your dick is little." India said with a smile and after that she didn't feel like being bothered anymore, so she went to tell her people's that she was leaving.

Once India got in the car to head home, her phone rang and she knew who it was right off the back.

"Yes Kevin." India said once she picked up the phone.

"Are you in the house?" Kevin asked.

"No, I'm at my parents' house. What's up?" India said.

"I was on my way over there to see you." Kevin said.

"Well, I'm not home and I don't feel like being bothered." India said really not in the mood for this. She just got some one minute, lame ass sex. All she wanted to do now was get something to eat, take a hot bath, and go to bed.

"Damn ma. I know what you need. You need me in your life and you know it, ma." Kevin said.

India was quiet for a minute because she wanted to see Kevin and get some of that good dick that he had, but she don't want to catch feelings for him. So she had to play cool.

"What makes you think I need you? I'll call you later because I'm busy."

"Alright ma, I'll be waiting. Don't try and play me either." Kevin said then hung up the phone.

India looked in her rearview mirror and said to herself "Girl, this man is really digging you. Keep playing the game cause you don't want to be a victim of his."

If you're interested in becoming an author for True Glory Publications, please submit three completed chapters to Trueg\lorypublications@gmail.com.

Other links released on Amazon by True Glory Publications:

Tiffany Stephens

Expect the Unexpected Part 1

http://www.amazon.com/Expect-Unexpected-Tiffany-Stephens-ebook/dp/B00J84URUM/ref=sr_1_1?ie=UTF8&qid=1413570346&sr=8-1&keywords=TIFFANY+STEPHENS

Expect the Unexpected Part 2

http://www.amazon.com/Expect-Unexpected-2-Tiffany-Stephens-ebook/dp/B00LHCCYG8/ref=sr_1_2?ie=UTF8&qid=1413570346&sr=8-2&keywords=TIFFANY+STEPHENS

Kim Morris: Tears I Shed Part 1 & 2

http://www.amazon.com/Tears-I-Shed-Kim-Morris/dp/1499319800

http://www.amazon.com/Tears-I-Shed-2-ebook/dp/B00N4FD03C

Sha Cole

Her Mother's Love Part 1

http://www.amazon.com/Her-Mothers-love-Sha-Cole-
ebook/dp/B00H93Z03I/ref=sr_1_1?s=digital-
text&ie=UTF8&qid=1405463882&sr=1-
1&keywords=her+mothers+love

Her Mother's Love Part 2

http://www.amazon.com/HER-MOTHERS-LOVE-Sha-
Cole-
ebook/dp/B00IKBGWW6/ref=pd_sim_kstore_1?ie=UTF8
&refRID=1EFA9EPXRPBSQPZVWHM0

Her Mother's Love Part 3

http://www.amazon.com/Her-Mothers-Love-Sha-Cole-
ebook/dp/B00L2SHLNI/ref=pd_sim_kstore_1?ie=UTF8&r
efRID=1AW831PBNBGAPPP9G8A9

Guessing Game

http://www.amazon.com/Guessing-Game-Sha-Cole-
ebook/dp/B00ODST1AA/ref=sr_1_8?ie=UTF8&qid=1413
041318&sr=8-8&keywords=Sha+Cole

Niki Jilvontae

A Broken Girl's Journey

http://www.amazon.com/BROKEN-GIRLS-JOURNEY-Niki-Jilvontae-ebook/dp/B00IICJRQK/ref=sr_1_5?ie=UTF8&qid=1413419382&sr=8-5&keywords=niki+jilvontae

A Broken Girl's Journey 2

http://www.amazon.com/BROKEN-GIRLS-JOURNEY-ebook/dp/B00J9ZM9YW/ref=sr_1_4?ie=UTF8&qid=1413419382&sr=8-4&keywords=niki+jilvontae

A Broken Girl's Journey 3

http://www.amazon.com/BROKEN-GIRLS-JOURNEY-ebook/dp/B00JVDFTBM/ref=sr_1_1?ie=UTF8&qid=1413419382&sr=8-1&keywords=niki+jilvontae

A Broken Girl's Journey 4: Kylie's Song

http://www.amazon.com/Broken-Girls-Journey-Kylies-Song-ebook/dp/B00NK89604/ref=sr_1_6?ie=UTF8&qid=1413419382&sr=8-6&keywords=niki+jilvontae

A Long Way from Home

http://www.amazon.com/Long-Way-Home-Niki-Jilvontae-
ebook/dp/B00LCN252U/ref=sr_1_3?ie=UTF8&qid=14134
19382&sr=8-3&keywords=niki+jilvontae

Your Husband, My Man Part 2 KC Blaze

http://www.amazon.com/Your-Husband-Man-YOUR-

HUSBAND-

ebook/dp/B00MUAKRPQ/ref=sr_1_1?ie=UTF8&qid=141

3593158&sr=8-1&keywords=your+husband+my+man+2

Your Husband, My Man Part 3 KC Blaze

http://www.amazon.com/Your-Husband-My-Man-3-

ebook/dp/B00OJODI8Y/ref=sr_1_1?ie=UTF8&qid=14135

93252&sr=8-

1&keywords=your+husband+my+man+3+kc+blaze

Child of a Crackhead I Shameek Speight

http://www.amazon.com/CHILD-CRACKHEAD-Part-1-ebook/dp/B0049U4W56/ref=sr_1_1?s=digital-text&ie=UTF8&qid=1413594876&sr=1-1&keywords=child+of+a+crackhead

Child of a Crackhead II Shameek Speight
http://www.amazon.com/CHILD-CRACKHEAD-II-Shameek-Speight-ebook/dp/B004MME12K/ref=sr_1_2?ie=UTF8&qid=1413593375&sr=8-2&keywords=child+of+a+crackhead+series

Pleasure of Pain Part 1 Shameek Speight
http://www.amazon.com/Pleasure-pain-Shameek-Speight-ebook/dp/B005C68BE4/ref=sr_1_1?s=digital-text&ie=UTF8&qid=1413593888&sr=1-1&keywords=pleasure+of+pain

Infidelity at its Finest Part 1 Kylar Bradshaw

http://www.amazon.com/INFIDELITY-AT-ITS-FINEST-

Book-ebook/dp/B00HV539A0/ref=sr_1_sc_1?s=digital-

text&ie=UTF8&qid=1413595045&sr=1-1-

spell&keywords=Infideltiy+at+its+finest

Infidelity at its Finest Part 2 Kylar Bradshaw

http://www.amazon.com/Infidelity-Finest-Part-Kylar-

Bradshaw-ebook/dp/B00IORHGNA/ref=sr_1_2?s=digital-

text&ie=UTF8&qid=1413593700&sr=1-

2&keywords=infidelity+at+its+finest

Marques Lewis

It's Love For Her part 1 http://www.amazon.com/Its-Love-
Her-Marques-Lewis-
ebook/dp/B00KAQAI1A/ref=la_B00B0GACDI_1_3?s=bo
oks&ie=UTF8&qid=1413647892&sr=1-3

It's Love For Her 2   http://www.amazon.com/Its-Love-For-Her-ebook/dp/B00KXLGG5O/ref=pd_sim_b_1?ie=UTF8&refRID=1ABE9DSRTHFFH13WGH6E

It's Love For Her 3 http://www.amazon.com/Its-Love-For-Her-ebook/dp/B00NUOIP0A/ref=pd_sim_kstore_1?ie=UTF8&refRID=1PYKVRTJJJMYCHE0P5RQ

Words of Wetness   http://www.amazon.com/Words-Wetness-Marques-Lewis-ebook/dp/B00MMQT2OU/ref=pd_sim_kstore_2?ie=UTF8&refRID=1FJFWTZSN2DBCV6PX3MG

He Loves Me to Death Sonovia Alexander

http://www.amazon.com/HE-LOVES-DEATH-LOVE-Book-ebook/dp/B00I2E1ARI/ref=sr_1_1?s=books&ie=UTF8&qid=1416789703&sr=1-1&keywords=sonovia+alexander

Silent Cries Sonovia Alexander

http://www.amazon.com/Silent-Cries-Sonovia-Alexander-ebook/dp/B00FANSOEQ/ref=sr_1_6?s=books&ie=UTF8&qid=1416789941&sr=1-6&keywords=sonovia+alexander+silent+cries

Ghetto Love Sonovia Alexander

http://www.amazon.com/GHETTO-LOVE-Sonovia-Alexander-ebook/dp/B00GK5AP5O/ref=sr_1_5?s=books&ie=UTF8&qid=1416790164&sr=1-5&keywords=sonovia+alexander+ghetto+love

Robert Cost

Every Bullet Gotta Name Part 1

http://www.amazon.com/dp/B00SU7KJ7O

Every Bullet Gotta Name Part 2

http://www.amazon.com/dp/B00TE7PSGG